"No, Sam. You don't get to stand there and pretend to know me."

"I do know you, Lacy," he argued, coming around the desk. "We were married."

"*Were* being the operative word," she reminded him. "You don't know me anymore. I've changed."

"I can see that. But the basics are the same. You still smell like lilacs. You still wear your hair in that thick braid I used to love to undo and spill across your shoulders..."

Lacy's stomach did a fast, jittery spin and her heartbeat leaped into a gallop. How was it fair that he could still make her body come alive with a few soft words and a heated look? Why hadn't the need for him drowned in the sea of hurt and anger that had enveloped her when he'd left?

AFTER HOURS
WITH HER EX

BY
MAUREEN CHILD

Published in Great Britain 2015
by Mills & Boon, an imprint of Harlequin (UK) Limited,
Eton House, 18-24 Paradise Road, Richmond, Surrey, TW9 1SR

© 2015 Maureen Child

ISBN: 978-0-263-25767-0

Harlequin (UK) Limited's policy is to use papers that are natural, renewable and recyclable products and made from wood grown in sustainable forests. The logging and manufacturing processes conform to the legal environmental regulations of the country of origin.

Printed and bound in Great Britain
by CPI Antony Rowe, Chippenham, Wiltshire

Maureen Child writes for the Mills & Boon® Desire™ line and can't imagine a better job. A seven-time finalist for the prestigious Romance Writers of America RITA® Award, Maureen is the author of more than one hundred romance novels. Her books regularly appear on bestseller lists and have won several awards, including a Prism Award, a National Readers' Choice Award, a Colorado Romance Writers Award of Excellence and a Golden Quill Award.

One of her books, *The Soul Collector*, was made into a CBS TV movie starring Melissa Gilbert, Bruce Greenwood and Ossie Davis. If you look closely, in the last five minutes of the movie you'll spot Maureen, who was an extra in the last scene.

Maureen believes that laughter goes hand in hand with love, so her stories are always filled with humor. The many letters she receives assure her that her readers love to laugh as much as she does. Maureen Child is a native Californian but has recently moved to the mountains of Utah.

One

"You actually *can* go home again," Sam Wyatt murmured as he stared at the main lodge of his family's resort. "The question is, will anyone be happy to see you."

But then, why should they be? He'd left Snow Vista, Utah, two years before, when his twin brother had died. And in walking away, he'd left his family to pick up the pieces strewn in the wake of Jack's death.

Guilt had forced Sam to leave. Had kept him away. And now, a different kind of guilt had brought him home again. Maybe it was time, he told himself. Time to face the ghosts that haunted this mountain.

The lodge looked the same. Rough-hewn logs, gray, weathered shingles and a wide front porch studded with Adirondack chairs fitted with jewel-toned cushions. The building itself was three stories; the Wyatt family had added that third level as family quarters just a few years ago. Guest rooms crowded the bottom two floors and there were a few cabins on the property as well, offering privacy along with a view that simply couldn't be beat.

Mostly, though, the tourists who came to ski at Snow Vista stayed in hotels a mile or so down the mountain. The Wyatt resort couldn't hold them all. A few years ago, Sam and his twin, Jack, had laid out plans for expanding the lodge, adding cabins and building the Wyatt holdings into the go-to place in the Utah mountains. Sam's parents, Bob and Connie, had been eager to expand, but from the looks of it, any idea of expansion had stopped when Sam left the mountain. But then, a lot of things had stopped, hadn't they?

His grip tightened on his duffel bag, and briefly Sam wished to hell he could as easily get ahold of the thoughts racing maniacally through his mind. Coming home wouldn't be easy. But the decision was made. Time to face the past.

"Sam!"

The voice calling his name was familiar. His sister, Kristi, headed right for him, walking in long brisk strides. She wore an electric blue parka and ski pants tucked into black boots trimmed with black fur at the tops. Her big blue eyes were flashing—and not in welcome. But hell, he told himself, he hadn't been expecting a parade, had he?

"Hi, Kristi."

"Hi?" She walked right up to him, tilted her head back and met his gaze with narrowed eyes. "That's the best you've got? 'Hi, Kristi'? After two years?"

He met her anger with cool acceptance. Sam had known what he would face when he came home and there was no time like the present to jump in and get some of it over with. "What would you like me to say?"

She snorted. "It's a little late to be asking me what

I want, isn't it? If you cared, you would have asked before you left in the first place."

Hard to argue that point. And his sister's expression told him it would be pointless to try even if he could. Remembering the way Kristi had once looked up to him and Jack, Sam realized it wasn't easy to accept that her hero worship phase was over. Of course, he'd pushed that phase over a cliff himself.

But this wasn't why he'd come home. He wasn't going to rehash old decisions. He'd done what he had to do back then, just as he was doing today.

"Back then, I would have told you not to go," Kristi was saying and as she stared up at him, Sam saw a film of tears cover her eyes. She blinked quickly, though, as if determined to keep those tears at bay—for which he was grateful. "You left us. Just walked away. Like none of us mattered to you anymore…"

He blew out a breath, dropped his duffel bag and shoved both hands through his hair. "Of course you mattered. All of you did. *Do.*"

"Easy to say, isn't it, Sam?"

Would it do any good to explain that he had thought about calling home all the time?

No, he told himself. Because he hadn't called. Hadn't been in touch at all—except for a couple of postcards letting them know where he happened to be at the time—until his mother had found a way to track him down in Switzerland last week.

He still wasn't sure how she'd found him. But Connie Wyatt was a force to be reckoned with when she had a goal in mind. Probably, she had called every hotel in the city until she'd tracked him down.

"Look, I'm not getting into this with you. Not right

now anyway. Not until I've seen Dad." He paused, then asked, "How is he?"

A flicker of fear darted across her eyes, then was swept away in a fresh surge of anger. "Alive. And the doctor says he's going to be fine. It's just sad that all it took to get you to come home was Dad having a heart attack."

This was going great.

Then it seemed her fury drained away as her voice dropped and her gaze shifted from him to the mountain. "It was scary. Mom was a rock, like always, but it was scary. Hearing that it was a warning made it a little better but now it feels like…"

Her words trailed off, but Sam could have finished that sentence for her. A warning simply meant that the family was now watching Bob as if he were a live grenade, waiting to see if he'd explode. Probably driving his father nuts.

"Anyway," she said, her voice snapping back to knifelike sharpness. "If you're expecting a big welcome, you're in for a disappointment. We're too busy to care."

"That's fine by me," he said, though damned if it didn't bother him to have his little sister be so dismissive. "I'm not here looking for forgiveness."

"Why are you here, then?"

He looked into his sister's eyes. "Because this is where I'm needed."

"You were needed two years ago, too," she said, and he heard the hurt in her voice this time.

"Kristi…"

She shook her head, plastered a hard smile on her face and said, "I've got a lesson in a few minutes. I'll talk to you later. If you're still here."

With that, she turned and left, headed for one of the

bunny runs where inexperienced skiers got their first introduction to the sport. Kristi had been one of the instructors here since she was fourteen. All of the Wyatt kids had grown up on skis, and teaching newbies had been part of the family business.

When she disappeared into the crowd, Sam turned for the main lodge. Well, he'd known when he decided to come home that it wasn't going to be easy. But then, nothing in the past two years had been easy, had it?

Head down, strides long, he walked toward home a lot slower than he had left it.

The lodge was as he remembered it.

When he left, the renovations had been almost finished, and now the place looked as though the changes had settled in and claimed their place. The front windows were wider; there were dozens of leather club chairs gathered in conversational groups and huddled in front of the stone hearth where a fire burned brightly.

It might be cold outside, with the wind and snow, but here in the lodge, there was warmth and welcome. He wondered if any of that would extend to him.

He waved to Patrick Hennessey, manning the reception desk, then skirted past the stairs and around the corner to the private elevator to the third floor. Sam took a breath, flipped open the numerical code box and punched in the four numbers he knew so well, half expecting the family to have changed the code after he left. They hadn't, though, and the door shushed open for him to step inside.

They'd installed the elevator a few years ago when they added the third story. This way, none of their guests accidentally gained access to the family's space and the Wyatt's kept their privacy. The short ride ended, the door swished open and Sam was suddenly standing in the family room.

He had time for one brief glance around the familiar surroundings. Framed family photos hung on the cream-colored walls alongside professional shots of the mountain in winter and springtime. Gleaming tables held handcrafted lamps and the low wood table set between twin burgundy leather sofas displayed a selection of magazines and books. Windows framed a wide view of the resort and a river-stone hearth on one wall boasted a fire that crackled and leaped with heat and light.

But it was the two people in the room who caught and held his attention. His mother was curled up in her favorite, floral upholstered chair, an open book on her lap. And his father, Sam saw with a sigh of relief, was sitting in his oversize leather club chair, his booted feet resting on a matching hassock. The flat-screen TV hanging over the fireplace was turned to an old Western movie.

On the long flight from Switzerland and during the time spent traveling from the airport to the lodge, all Sam had been able to think about was his father having a heart attack. Sure, he'd been told that Bob Wyatt was all right and had been released from the hospital. But he hadn't really allowed himself to believe it until now.

Seeing the big man where he belonged, looking as rugged and larger than life as usual, eased that last, cold knot in the pit of Sam's stomach.

"Sam!" Connie Wyatt tossed her book onto a side table, jumped to her feet and raced across the room to him. She threaded her arms around him and held on tightly, as if preventing him from vanishing again. "Sam, you're here." She tipped her head back to smile up at him. "It's so good to see you."

He smiled back at her and realized how much he'd missed her and the rest of the family. For two years, Sam had been a gypsy, traveling from one country to another, chasing the next experience. He'd lived out of the duffel bag he still held tightly and hadn't looked any further ahead than the next airport or train connection.

He'd done some skiing of course. Sam didn't compete professionally anymore, but he couldn't go too long without hitting the slopes. Skiing was in his blood, even when he spent most of his time building his business. Designing ski runs at some of the top resort destinations in the world. The skiwear company he and Jack had begun was thriving as well, and between those two businesses, he'd managed to keep busy enough to not do much thinking.

Now he was here, meeting his father's studying gaze over the top of his mother's head. It was both surreal and right.

With a deliberate move, he dropped the duffel bag, then wrapped both arms around his much-shorter mother and gave her a hard hug. "Hi, Mom."

She pushed back, gave his chest a playful slap and shook her head. "I can't believe you're really here. You must be hungry. I'll go fix you something—"

"You don't have to do that," he said, knowing nothing could stop her. Connie Wyatt treated all difficult situations as a reason to feed people.

"Won't be a minute," she said, then shot her husband a quick glance. "I'll bring us all some coffee, too. You stay in that chair, mister."

Bob Wyatt waved one hand at his wife, but kept his gaze fixed on his son. As Connie rushed out of the room and headed for the family kitchen, Sam walked over to his father and took a seat on the footstool in front of him. "Dad. You look good."

Scowling, the older man brushed his gray-streaked hair back from his forehead and narrowed the green eyes he'd bequeathed to his sons. "I'm fine. Doctor says it wasn't anything. Just too much stress."

Stress. Because he'd lost one son, had another disappear on him and was forced to do most of the running of the family resort himself. Guilt Sam didn't want to acknowledge pinged him again as he realized that leaving the way he did had left everyone scrambling.

Frowning more deeply, his father looked over to the doorway where his wife had disappeared. "Your mother's bound and determined to make me an invalid, though."

"You scared her," Sam said. "Hell, you scared me."

His father watched him for several long minutes before saying, "Well now, you did some scaring of your own a couple years ago. Taking off, not letting us know where you were or how you were…"

Sam took a breath and blew it out. And there was the guilt again, settling back onto his shoulders like an unwelcome guest. It had been with him so long now, Sam thought he would probably never get rid of it entirely.

"Couple of postcards just weren't enough, son."

"I couldn't call," Sam said, and knew it sounded cowardly. "Couldn't hear your voices. Couldn't—hell, Dad. I was a damn mess."

"You weren't the only one hurting, Sam."

"I know that," he said, and felt a flicker of shame. "I do. But losing Jack…" Sam scowled at the memory as if that action alone could push it so far out of sight he'd never have to look at it again.

"He was your twin," Bob mused. "But he was our child. Just as you and Kristi are."

There it was. Sam had to accept that he'd caused his parents more pain at a time when they had already had more than enough loss to deal with. But back then, there had seemed to Sam to be only one answer.

"I had to go."

One short sentence that encapsulated the myriad emotions that had driven him from his home, his family.

"I know that." His father's gaze was steady and there was understanding there as well as sorrow. "Doesn't mean I have to like it, but I understand. Still, you're back now. For how long?"

He'd been expecting that question. The problem was, he didn't have an answer for it yet. Sam ducked his head briefly, then looked at his father again. "I don't know."

"Well," the older man said sadly, "that's honest at least."

"I can tell you," Sam assured him, "that this time I'll let you know before I leave. I can promise not to disappear again."

Nodding, his father said, "Then I guess that'll have to do. For now." He paused and asked, "Have you seen... anyone else yet?"

"No. Just Kristi." Sam stiffened. There were still minefields to step through. Hard feelings and pain to be faced. There was no way out but through.

As hard as it was to face his family, he'd chosen to see them first, because what was still to come would be far more difficult.

"Well then," his father spoke up, "you should know that—"

The elevator swished open. Sam turned to face whoever was arriving and instantly went still as stone. He hardly heard his father complete the sentence that had been interrupted.

"—Lacy's on her way over here."

Lacy Sills.

She stood just inside the room, clutching at a basket of muffins that filled the room with a tantalizing scent. Sam's heart gave one hard lurch in his chest. She looked good. Too damn good.

She stood five foot eight and her long blond hair hung in a single thick braid over her left shoulder. Her navy blue coat was unbuttoned to reveal a heavy, fisherman's knit, forest-green sweater over her black jeans. Her boots were black, too, and came to her knees. Her features were the same: a generous mouth; a straight, small nose; and blue eyes the color of deep summer. She didn't smile. Didn't speak. And didn't have to.

In a split second, blood rushed from his head to his lap and just like that, he was hard as a rock. Lacy had always had that effect on him.

That's why he'd married her.

Lacy couldn't move. Couldn't seem to draw a breath past the tight knot of emotion lodged in her throat. Her heartbeat was too fast and she felt a head rush, as if she'd had one too many glasses of wine.

She should have called first. Should have made sure the Wyatts were alone here at the lodge. But then, her mind argued, why should she? It wasn't as if she'd expected to see Sam sitting there opposite his father. And now that she had, she was determined to hide her reaction to him. After all, she wasn't the one who'd walked out on her family. Her *life*. She'd done nothing to be ashamed of.

Except of course, for missing him. Her insides were

jumping, her pulse raced and an all too familiar swirl of desire spun in the pit of her stomach. How was it possible that she could still feel so much for a man who had tossed her aside without a second thought?

When Sam left, she had gone through so many different stages of grief, she had thought she'd never come out the other side of it all. But she had. Finally.

How was it fair that he was here again when she was just getting her life back?

"Hello, Lacy."

His voice was the deep rumble of an avalanche forming and she knew that, to her, it held the same threat of destruction. He was watching her out of grass-green eyes she had once gotten lost in. And he looked so darn good. Why did he have to look so good? By all rights, he should be covered in boils and blisters as punishment for what he'd done.

Silence stretched out until it became a presence in the room. She had to speak. She couldn't just stand there. Couldn't let him know what it cost her to meet his gaze.

"Hello, Sam," she finally managed to say. "It's been a while."

Two years. Two years of no word except for a few lousy postcards sent to his parents. He'd never contacted Lacy. Never let her know he was sorry. That he missed her. That he wished he hadn't gone. Nothing. She'd spent countless nights worrying about whether he was alive or dead. Wondering why she should care either way. Wondering when the pain of betrayal and abandonment would stop.

"Lacy." Bob Wyatt spoke up and held out one hand toward her. In welcome? Or in the hope that she wouldn't bolt?

Lacy's spine went poker straight. She wouldn't run.

This mountain was her home. She wouldn't be chased away by the very man who had run from everything he'd loved.

"Did you bake me something?" Bob asked. "Smells good enough to eat."

Grateful for the older man's attempt to help her through this oh-so-weird situation, Lacy gave him a smile as she took a deep, steadying breath. In the past two years, she had spent a lot of nights figuring out how she would handle herself when she first saw Sam again. Now it was time to put all of those mental exercises into practice.

She would be cool, calm. She would never let on that simply looking at him made everything inside her weep for what they'd lost. And blast it, she would never let him know just how badly he'd broken her heart.

Forcing a smile she didn't quite feel, she headed across the room, looking only at Bob, her father-in-law. That's how she thought of him still, despite the divorce that Sam had demanded. Bob and Connie Wyatt had been family to Lacy since she was a girl, and she wasn't about to let that end just because their son was a low-down miserable excuse for a man.

"I did bake, just for you," she said, setting the basket in Bob's lap and bending down to plant a quick kiss on the older man's forehead. "Your favorite, cranberry-orange."

Bob took a whiff, sighed and gave her a grin. "Girl, you are a wonder in the kitchen."

"And *you* are a sucker for sugar," she teased.

"Guilty as charged." He glanced from her to Sam. "Why don't you sit down, visit for a while? Connie went off to get some snacks. Join us."

They used to all gather together in this room and

there was laughter and talking and a bond she had thought was stronger than anything. Those times were gone, though. Besides, with Sam sitting there watching her, Lacy's stomach twisted, making even the thought of food a hideous one to contemplate. Now, a gigantic glass of wine, on the other hand, was a distinct possibility.

"No, but thanks. I've got to get out to the bunny run. I've got lessons stacked up for the next couple of hours."

"If you're sure…" Bob's tone told her he knew exactly why she was leaving and the compassion in his eyes let her know he understood.

Oh, if he started being sympathetic, this could get ugly fast and she wasn't about to let a single tear drop anywhere in the vicinity of Sam Wyatt. She'd already done enough crying over him to last a lifetime. Blast if she'd put on a personal show for him!

"I'm sure," she said quickly. "But I'll come back tomorrow to check on you."

"That'd be good," Bob told her and gave her hand a pat.

Lacy didn't even look at Sam as she turned for the elevator. Frankly, she wasn't sure what she might do or say if she met those green eyes again. Better to just go about her life—teaching little kids and their scared mamas to ski. Then she'd go home, have that massive glass of wine, watch some silly chick flick and cry to release all of the tears now clogging her throat. Right now, though, all she wanted was to get out of there as quickly as she could.

But she should have known her tactic wouldn't work.

"Lacy, wait."

Sam was right behind her—she heard his footsteps on the wood floor—but she didn't stop. Didn't dare. She made it to the elevator and stabbed at the button.

But even as the door slid open, Sam's hand fell onto her shoulder.

That one touch sent heat slicing through her and she hissed in a breath in an attempt to keep that heat from spreading. Deliberately, she dipped down, escaping his touch, then stepped into the elevator.

Sam slapped one hand onto the elevator door to keep it open as he leaned toward her. "Damn it, Lacy, we have to talk."

"Why?" she countered. "Because you say so? No, Sam. We have nothing to talk about."

"I'm—"

Her head snapped up and she glared at him. "And so help me, if you say 'I'm sorry,' I will find a way to make sure you are."

"You're not making this easy," he remarked.

"Oh, you mean like you did, two years ago?" Despite her fury, she kept her voice a low hiss. She didn't want to upset Bob.

God, she hadn't wanted to get into this at all. She never wanted to talk about the day Sam had handed her divorce papers and then left the mountain—and *her*—behind.

Deliberately keeping her gaze fixed to his, she punched the button for the lobby. "I have to work. Let go of the door."

"You're going to have to talk to me at some point."

She reached up, pulled his fingers off the cold steel and as the door closed quietly, she assured him, "No, Sam. I really don't."

Two

Thank God, Lacy thought, for the class of toddlers she was teaching. It kept her so busy she didn't have time to think about Sam. Or about what it might mean having him back home.

But because her mind was occupied didn't mean that her body hadn't gone into a sort of sense memory celebration. Even her skin seemed to recall what it felt like when Sam touched her. And every square inch of her buzzed with anticipation.

"Are you sure it's safe to teach her how to ski so soon?" A woman with worried brown eyes looked from Lacy to her three-year-old daughter, struggling to stay upright on a pair of tiny skis.

"Absolutely," Lacy answered, pushing thoughts of Sam to the back of her mind, where she hoped they would stay. If her body was looking forward to being with Sam again, it would just have to deal with disappointment. "My father started me off at two. When you begin this young, there's no fear. Only a sense of adventure."

The woman laughed a little. "That I understand." Her gaze lifted to the top of the lift at the mountain's summit. "I've got plenty of fear, but my husband loves skiing so…"

Lacy smiled as she watched her assistant help a little boy up from where he'd toppled over into the soft, powdery snow. "You'll love it. I promise."

"Hope so," she said wistfully. "Right now, Mike's up there somewhere—" she pointed at the top of the mountain "—with his brother. He's going to watch Kaylee while I have my lesson this afternoon."

"Kristi Wyatt's teaching your class," Lacy told her. "And she's wonderful. You'll enjoy it. Really."

The woman's gaze swung back to her. "The Wyatt family. My husband used to come here on ski trips just to watch the Wyatt brothers ski."

Lacy's smile felt a little stiff, but she gave herself points for keeping it in place. "A lot of people did."

"It was just tragic what happened to Jack Wyatt."

The woman wasn't the first person to bring up the past, and no doubt she wouldn't be the last, either. Even two years after Jack's death, his fans still came to Snow Vista in a sort of pilgrimage. He hadn't been forgotten. Neither had Sam. In the skiing world, the Wyatt twins had been, and always would be, rock stars.

The woman's eyes were kind, sympathetic and yet, curious. Of course she was. Everyone remembered Jack Wyatt, champion skier, and everyone knew how Jack's story had ended.

What they didn't know was what that pain had done to the family left behind. Two years ago, it had been all

Lacy could think about. She'd driven herself half-crazy asking herself the kind of what-if questions that had no answers, only possibilities. And those possibilities had haunted her. Had kept her awake at night, alone in her bed. She'd wondered and cried and wondered again until her emotions were wrung out and she was left with only a sad reality staring her in the face.

Jack had died, but it was the people he'd left behind who had suffered.

"Yes," Lacy agreed, feeling her oh-so-tight smile slipping away. "It was." And tragic that the ripple effect of what happened to Jack had slammed its way through the Wyatt family like an avalanche, wiping out everything in its path.

While the kids practiced and Lacy's assistant supervised, the woman continued in a hushed voice. "My husband keeps up with everything even mildly related to the skiing world. He said that Jack's twin, Sam, left Snow Vista after his brother's death."

God, how could Lacy get out of this conversation?

"Yes, he did."

"Apparently, he left competitive skiing and he's some kind of amazing ski resort designer now and he's got a line of ski equipment and he's apparently spent the last couple of years dating royalty in Europe."

Lacy's heart gave one vicious tug and she took a deep breath, hoping to keep all the emotions churning inside her locked away. It wasn't easy. After all, though Sam hadn't contacted the family except for the occasional postcard, he was a high-profile athlete with a tragic past who got more than his share of media attention.

So it hadn't been difficult to keep up with what he'd been doing the past couple of years. Lacy knew all about his businesses and how he'd put his name on everything from goggles to ski poles. He was rich, famous and gorgeous. Of course the media was all over him. So naturally, Lacy had been treated to paparazzi photos of Sam escorting beautiful women to glamorous events—and yes, he had been photographed with a dark-haired, skinny countess who looked as though she hadn't had a regular meal in ten years.

But it didn't matter what he did, because Sam was Lacy's *ex*-husband. So they could both date whomever they wanted to. Not that she had dated much—or any for that matter. But she could if she wanted to and that's what mattered.

"Do you actually know the Wyatts?" the woman asked, then stopped and caught herself. "Silly question. Of course you do. You work for them."

True. And up until two years ago, Lacy had been one of them. But that was another life and this was the one she had to focus on.

"Yes, I do," Lacy said, forcing another smile she didn't feel. "And speaking of work, I should really get to today's lessons."

Then she walked to join her assistant Andi and the group of kids who demanded nothing but her time.

Sam waited for hours.

He kept an eye on Lacy's classes and marveled that she could be so patient—not just with the kids but with the hovering parents who seemed to have an opinion on everything that happened. She hadn't changed, he thought with some small satisfaction. She was still patient, reasonable. But then, Lacy had always been the calm one. The cool head that invariably had smoothed over any trouble that rose up between Sam and Jack.

He and his twin had argued over everything, and

damned if Sam didn't still miss it. A twinge pulled at his heart and he ignored it as he had for the past two years. Memories clamored in the back of his mind and he ignored them, as well. He'd spent too much time burying all reminders of the pain that had chased him away from his home.

Muttering under his breath, he shoved one hand through his hair and focused on the woman he hadn't been able to forget. She hadn't changed, he thought again and found that intriguing as well as comforting. The stir of need and desire inside him thickened into a hot flow like lava through his veins.

That hadn't changed, either.

"Okay, that's it for today," Lacy was saying and the sound of her voice rippled along his spine like a touch.

Sam shook his head to clear it of any thoughts that would get in the way of the conversation he was about to have and then he waited.

"Parents," Lacy called out with a smile, "thanks for trusting us with your children. And if you want to sign up for another lesson, just see my assistant Andi and she'll take care of it."

Andi was new, Sam thought, barely glancing at the young woman with the bright red hair and a face full of freckles. His concentration was fixed on Lacy. As if she felt his focused stare, she lifted her head and met his gaze over the heads of the kids gathered around her.

She tore her gaze from his, smiled and laughed with the kids, and then slowly made her way to him. He watched every step. Her long legs looked great in black jeans and the heavy sweater she wore clung to a figure he remembered all too well.

Despite the snow covering the ground and the surrounding pines, the sun shone brilliantly out of a bright blue sky, making the air warm in spite of the snow. Lacy flipped her long blond braid over her shoulder to lie down the center of her back and never slowed her steps until she was right in front of him.

"Sam."

"Lacy, we need to talk."

"I already told you we have nothing to say to each other."

She tried to brush past him, but he caught her arm in a firm grip and kept her at his side. Her gaze snapped to his hand and made her meaning clear. He didn't care. If anything, he tightened his hold on her.

"Time to clear the air," he said softly, mindful of the fact that there was a huge crowd ebbing and flowing around them.

"That's funny coming from you," she countered. "I don't remember you wanting to talk two years ago. All I remember is seeing you walk away. Oh, yeah. And I remember divorce papers arriving two weeks later. You didn't want to talk then. Why all of a sudden are you feeling chatty?"

He stared at her, a little stunned at her response. Not that it wasn't justified; it was only that the Lacy he remembered never would have said any of it. She was always so controlled. So…soft.

"You've changed some," he mused.

"If you mean I speak for myself now, then yes. I have changed. Enough that I don't want to go back to who I was then—easily breakable."

He clenched his jaw at the accusation that *he* had been the one to break her. Sam could admit that he'd handled everything badly two years ago, but if she was so damaged, how was she standing there glaring at him?

"Looks to me like you recovered nicely," he pointed out.

"No thanks to you." She glanced around, as if to make sure no one could overhear them.

"You're right about that," he acknowledged. "But we still have to talk."

Staring into his eyes now, she said, "Because you say so? Sorry, Sam. Not how it works. You can't disappear for two years, then drop back in and expect me to roll over and do whatever it is you want."

Her voice was cool, and her eyes were anything but. He could see sparks of indignation in those blue depths that surprised him. The new attitude also came with a temper. But then, she had every right to be furious. She was still going to listen to him.

"Lacy," he ground out, "I'm here now. We'll have to see each other every day."

"Not if I can help it," she countered, and the flash in her eyes went bright.

Around them, the day went on. Couples walked hand in hand. Parents herded children and squeals of excitement sliced through the air. Up on the mountain, skiers in a rainbow of brightly colored parkas raced down the slopes.

Here, though, Sam was facing a challenge of a different kind. She'd been in his thoughts and dreams for two years. Soft, sweet, trusting. Yet this new side of Lacy appealed to him, too. He liked the fire sparking in her eyes, even if it was threatening to engulf him.

When she tugged to get free of his grip, he let her go, but his fingertips burned as if he'd been holding on to a live electrical wire. "Lacy, you work for me—"

"I work for your father," she corrected.

"You work for the Wyatts," he reminded her. "I'm a Wyatt."

Her head snapped up and those furious blue eyes narrowed to slits. "And you're the one Wyatt I want nothing to do with."

"Lacy?"

Kristi's voice came from right behind him and Sam bit back an oath. His sister had lousy timing was his first thought, then he realized that she was interrupting on purpose. As if riding to Lacy's rescue.

"Hi, Kristi." Lacy gave her a smile and blatantly ignored Sam's presence. "You need something?"

"Actually, yeah." Kristi gave her brother one long, hard look, then turned back to Lacy. "If you're not busy, I'd like to go over some of the plans for next weekend's End of Season ski party."

"I'm not busy at all." Lacy gave Sam a meaningful look. "We were done here, right?"

If he said no, he'd have two angry women to face. If he said yes, Lacy would believe that he was willing to step away from the confrontation they needed to have—which he wasn't. Yeah, two years ago he'd walked away. But he was back now and they were both going to have to find a way to deal with it.

For however long he was here.

"For now," he finally said, and saw the shimmer of relief in Lacy's eyes. It would be short-lived, though, because the two of them weren't finished.

After Lacy and Kristi left, Sam wandered the resort, familiarizing himself with it all. He could have drawn the place from memory—from the bunny runs to the slalom courses to the small snack shops. And yet, after being gone for two years, Sam was looking at the place through new eyes.

He'd been making some changes to the resort, beginning the expansion he'd once dreamed of, when Jack died. Then, like a light switch flipping off, his dreams for the place had winked out of existence. Sam frowned and stared up at the top of the mountain. There were other resorts in Utah. Big ones, small ones, each of them drawing away a slice of tourism skiing that Snow Vista should be able to claim.

While he looked around, his mind worked. They needed more cabins for guests. Maybe another inn, separate from the hotel. A restaurant at the summit. Something that offered more substantial fare than hot dogs and popcorn. And for serious skiers, they needed to open a run on the backside of the mountain where the slope was sheer and there were enough trees and jumps to make for a dangerous—and exciting—run.

God knew he had more than enough money to invest in Snow Vista. All it would take was his father's approval, and why the hell wouldn't he go for it? With work and some inventive publicity, Sam could turn Snow Vista into the premier ski resort in the country.

But to make all of these changes would mean that he'd have to stay. To dig his heels in and reclaim the life that he'd once walked away from. And he wasn't sure he wanted to do that. Or that he could. He wasn't the same man who had left here two years ago. He'd changed as much as Lacy had. Maybe more.

Staying here would mean accepting everything he'd once run from. It would mean living with Jack's ghost. Seeing him on every ski run. Hearing his laugh on the wind.

Sam's gaze fixed on a lone skier making his way

down the mountain. Snow flared up from the sides of his skis and as he bent low to pick up speed, Sam could almost feel the guy's exhilaration. Sam had grown up on that mountain and just seeing it again was easing all of the rough edges on his soul that he'd been carrying around for two years. It wouldn't be easy, but he belonged here. A part of him always would.

And just like that, he knew that he would stay. At least as long as it took to make all of the changes he'd once dreamed of making to his family's resort.

The first step on that journey was laying it out for his father.

"And you want to oversee all of this yourself?"

"Yeah," Sam said, leaning back in one of the leather chairs in the family great room. "I do. We can make Snow Vista the place everyone wants to come."

"You've only been back a couple hours." Bob's eyes narrowed on his son. "You're not taking much more time over this decision than you did with the one to leave."

Sam shifted in his chair. He'd made his choice. He just needed to convince his father that it was the right one.

"You sure you want to do this?"

The decision had come easily. Quickly, even though he'd barely arrived. Maybe he should take some time. Settle in. Determine if this was what he really wanted to do. But even as he considered it, he dismissed it.

Looking at his father, Sam realized that his first concern—the worry that had brought him home—had been eased. His dad was in no danger. His health wasn't deteriorating. But still, the old man would have to rest up, take it easy, which meant that Sam was needed here. At least for the time being.

And if he didn't involve himself in the family resort, what the hell would he do with himself while he was here? He scrubbed one hand across the back of his neck. If he got right to work he could have most of the changes made and completed within a few months. By then, his dad should be up and feeling himself again and Sam could... "Yeah, Dad. I'm sure I want to do it. If I get started right away, most of it can be finished within a few months."

"I remember you and Jack sitting up half the night with drawings and notebooks, planning out what you were going to do to the place." His father sighed heavily and Sam could feel his pain. But then his father nodded, tapped the fingers of his right hand against his knee. "You'll supervise it all? Take charge?"

"I will." Heat swarmed through the room, rushing from the hearth where a fire burned with licks and hisses of flames.

"So this means you're staying?" His father's gaze was wise and steady and somehow way too perceptive.

"I'll stay. Until I've got everything done anyway." That was all he could promise. All he could swear to.

"Could take months."

"To finish everything? I figure at least six," Sam agreed.

His father shifted his gaze to stare out the window at the sprawling view of the Salt Lake Valley. "I shouldn't let you put your money on the line," he finally said quietly. "You've got your own life now."

"I'm still a Wyatt," Sam said easily.

Bob slowly turned his head to look at his son. "Glad to hear you remember that."

Guilt poked at Sam again and he didn't care for it. Hell, until two years ago, guilt had never been a part of his life, but since then, it had been his constant companion. "I remember."

"Took you long enough," his father said softly. "We missed you here."

"I know, Dad." He leaned forward, braced his elbows on his knees and let his hands hang in front of him. "But I had to go. Had to get away from—"

"Us."

Sam's head snapped up and his gaze fixed on his father's face, wreathed in sorrow. "No, Dad. I wasn't trying to get away from the family. I was trying to lose myself."

"Not real smart," the older man mused, "since you took you with you when you left."

"Yeah," Sam muttered, jumping to his feet and pacing. His father's point made perfect sense when said out loud like that. But two years ago, Sam hadn't been willing or able to listen to anyone. He hadn't wanted advice. Or sympathy. He'd only wanted space. Between himself and everything that reminded him he was alive and his twin was dead.

He stalked back and forth across the wide floor until he finally came to a stop in front of the man sitting quietly, watching him. "At the time, it seemed like the only thing to do. After Jack…" He shook his head and bit back words that were useless.

Didn't matter now why he'd done what he had. Hearing him say that he regretted his choices wouldn't change the fact that he had walked out on the people who loved him. Needed him. But they, none of them, could understand what it had meant when his twin— the other half of himself—had died.

His dad nodded glumly. "Losing Jack took a huge chunk out of this family. Tore us all to pieces, you more than the rest of us, I'm guessing. But putting all that aside, I need to know, Sam. If you start something here, I need to know you'll stay to see it through."

"I give you my word, Dad. I'll stay till it's done."

"That's good enough for me," his father said, and pushed out of his chair. Standing, he offered his hand to Sam and when they shook on it, Bob Wyatt smiled and said, "You'll have to work with our resort manager to get this up and running."

Sam nodded. Their resort manager had been with the Wyatts for twenty years. "Dave Mendez. I'll see him tomorrow."

"Guess you haven't heard yet. Dave retired last year."

"What?" Surprised, Sam asked, "Well who replaced him?"

His father gave him a wide grin. "Lacy Sills."

First thing the next morning, Lacy was sipping a latte as she opened the door to her office. She nearly choked on the swallow of hot milk and espresso. Gasping for air, she slapped one hand on her chest and glared at the man sitting behind *her* desk.

"What're you doing here?"

Sam took his time looking up from the sheaf of papers in front of him. "I'm going over the reports for the hotel, the cabins and the snack bar. Haven't gotten to the ski runs yet, but I will."

"Why?" She managed one word, her fingers tightening on the paper cup in her hand.

God, it was a wonder she could think, let alone talk. Her head was fuzzed out and her brain hadn't quite clicked into top gear. It was all Kristi's fault, Lacy told herself. Sam's sister had come over to Lacy's cabin the night before, carrying two bottles of wine and a huge platter of brownies.

At the time it had seemed like a great idea. Getting a little drunk with her oldest friend. Talking trash about the man who was such a central part in both of their lives.

Sam.

It always came down to Sam, she thought and wished to heaven she had a clear enough head to be on top of this situation. But, she thought sadly, even without a hangover, she wouldn't be at her best facing the man who had shattered her heart.

It was still hard for her to believe that he'd come back. Even harder to know what to do about it. The safest thing, she knew, would be to keep her distance. To avoid him as much as possible and to remind herself often that no doubt he'd be leaving again. He had left, he said at the time, because he hadn't been able to face living with the memories of Jack.

Nothing had changed.

Which meant that Sam wouldn't stay.

And Lacy would do whatever she had to, to keep from being broken again.

"When I left," Sam said quietly, "we had just started making changes around here."

"Yes, I remember." She edged farther into the office, but the room on the first floor of the Wyatt lodge was a small one and every step she took brought her closer to *him*. "We finished the reno to the lodge, but once that was done, we put off most of the rest. Your folks just weren't…" Her voice trailed off.

The Wyatts hadn't been in the mood to change anything after Jack's death changed *everything*.

"Well, while I'm here, we're going to tackle the rest of the plans."

While he was here.

That was plain enough, Lacy thought. He was making himself perfectly clear. "You talked to your dad about this?"

"Yeah." Sam folded his hands atop his flat abdomen and watched her. "He's good with it so we're going to get moving as quickly as possible."

"On what exactly?"

"For starters," he said, sitting forward again and picking up a single piece of paper, "we're going to expand the snack bar at the top of the lift. I want a real restaurant up there. Something that will draw people in, make them linger for a while."

"A restaurant." She thought of the spot he meant and had to admit it was a good idea. Hot dogs and popcorn only appealed to so many people. "That's a big start."

"No point in staying small, is there?"

"I suppose not," she said, leaning back against the wall, clutching her latte cup hard enough she was surprised she hadn't crushed it in her fist. "What else?"

"We'll be building more cabins," he told her. "People like the privacy of their own space."

"They do."

"Glad you agree," he said with a sharp nod.

"Is there more?" she asked.

"Plenty," he said and waved one hand at the chair in front of the desk. "Sit down and we'll talk about it."

A spurt of anger shot through her. He had commandeered her office and her desk and now she was being relegated to the visitor's chair. A subtle move for power?

Shaking her head, she dropped into the seat and

looked at the man sitting opposite her. He was watching her as if he knew exactly what she was thinking.

"We're going to be working together on this, Lacy," he said quietly. "I hope that's not going to be a problem."

"I can do my job, Sam," she assured him.

"So can I, Lacy," he said. "The question is, can we do the job together?"

Three

It went wrong right from the jump. For the next hour, they butted heads continuously until Lacy had a headache the size of Idaho.

"You closed the intermediate run on the east side of the mountain," he said, glancing up from the reports. "I want that opened up again."

"We can't open it until next season," Lacy said, pausing for a sip of the latte that had gone cold over the past hour.

He dropped a pen onto the desk top. "And why's that?"

She met his almost-accusatory stare with cool indifference. "We had a storm come through late December. Tore down a few pines and dropped a foot and a half of snow." She crossed her legs and held her latte between her palms. "The pines are blocking the run and we can't get a crew in there to clear it out because the snow in the pass is too deep."

He frowned. "You waited too long to send in a crew."

At the insinuation of incompetence in his voice, she stood up and stared down at him. "I waited until the storm passed," she argued. "Once we got a look at the damage and I factored in the risks to the guys of clearing it, I closed that run."

Leaning back in his chair, he met her gaze. "So you ran the rest of the season on half power."

"We did fine," she said tightly. "Check the numbers."

"I have." Almost lazily, he stood so that he loomed over her, forcing her to lift her gaze. "You didn't do badly…"

"Thanks so much." Sarcasm dripped from every word.

"It would have been a better season with that run open."

"Well yeah," she said, setting her latte cup onto *her* desk. "But we don't always get what we want, do we?"

His eyes narrowed and she gave herself a mental pat on the back for that well-aimed barb. Before Sam had walked out on her and everyone else, she couldn't remember a time when she'd lost her temper. Now that he was back, though, the anger she used to keep tamped down kept bubbling up.

"Leaving that alone for the moment," he said, "the revenue from the snack bar isn't as high as it used to be."

She shrugged. This was not news to her. "Not that many people are interested in hot dogs, really. Most people go for a real lunch in town."

"Which is why building a restaurant at the summit is important," he said.

She hated that he was right. "I agree."

A half smile curved his mouth briefly and her stomach gave a quick twist in response. It was involuntary, she consoled herself. Sam smiled; she quivered. Didn't mean she had to let him know.

"If we can agree on one thing, there may be more."

"Don't count on it," she warned.

He tipped his head to one side and stared at her. "I don't remember you being so stubborn. Or having a temper."

"I learned how to stand up for myself while you were gone, Sam," she told him, lifting her chin to emphasize her feelings on this. "I won't smile and nod just because Sam Wyatt says something. When I disagree, you'll know it."

Nodding, he said, "I think I like the new Lacy as much as I did the old one. You're a strong woman. Always have been, whether you ever chose to show it or not."

"No," Lacy said softly. "You don't get to do that, Sam. You don't get to stand there and pretend to know me."

"I do know you, Lacy," he argued, coming around the desk. "We were married."

"*Were* being the operative word in that sentence," she reminded him, and took two steps back. "You don't know me anymore. I've changed."

"I can see that. But the basics are the same," he said, closing the distance between them again. "You still smell like lilacs. You still wear your hair in that thick braid I used to love to undo and spill across your shoulders…"

Lacy's stomach did a fast, jittery spin and her heartbeat leaped into a gallop. How was it fair that he could still make her body come alive with a few soft words and a heated look? Why hadn't the need for him drowned in the sea of hurt and anger that had enveloped her when he left?

"Stop it."

"Why?" He shook his head and kept coming, one long, slow step after another. "You're still beautiful. And I like the way temper makes your eyes flash."

The office just wasn't big enough for this, Lacy told herself, and crowded around behind the desk, trying to keep the solid piece of furniture between them. She didn't trust herself around him. Never had been able to. From the time she was a girl, she had wanted Sam and that feeling had never left her. Not even when he'd broken her heart by abandoning her.

"You don't have the right to talk to me like that now. You left, Sam. And I moved on."

Liar, her mind screamed. She hadn't moved on. How could she? Sam Wyatt was the love of her life. He was the only man she had ever wanted. The only one she still wanted, damn it. But he wasn't going to know that.

Because she had trusted him. More than anyone in her life, she had trusted him and he'd left her without a backward glance. The pain of that hadn't faded.

He narrowed his gaze on her. "There's someone else?"

She laughed, but the sharp edge of it scraped her throat. "Why do you sound so surprised? You've been gone two years, Sam. Did you think I'd enter a convent or something? That I'd throw myself on our torn-up marriage certificate and vow to never love another man?"

His jaw tightened, the muscle there twitching as he ground his teeth together. "Who is he?"

She sucked in a gulp of air. "None of your business."

"I hate that. But yeah, it's not," he agreed, moving

closer. So close that Lacy couldn't draw a breath without taking the scent of him—his shampoo, the barest hint of a foresty cologne—deep into her lungs. He looked the same. He felt the same. But *nothing* was the same.

Lacy felt the swirl of need she always associated with Sam. No other man affected her as he did. No other man had ever tempted her into believing in forever. And look how that had turned out.

"Sam." The window was at her back, the glass cold through her sweater and still doing nothing to chill the heat that pulsed inside her.

"Who is he, Lacy?" He reached up and fingered the end of her braid. "Do I know him?"

"No," she muttered, looking for a way out and not finding one. She could slip to the side, but he'd only move with her. Too close. She took another breath. "Why does it matter, Sam? Why would you care?"

"Like I said, we were married once," he said as if he had to remind her.

"We're not now," she told him flatly.

"No," he said, then lifted his fingers to tip up her chin, drawing her gaze to meet his. "Your eyes are still so damn blue."

His whisper shivered inside her. His touch sent bolts of heat jolting through her and Lacy took another breath to steady herself and instead was swamped by his scent, filling her, fogging her mind, awakening memories she'd worked so hard to bury.

"Do you taste the same?" he wondered softly, and lowered his head to hers.

She should stop him, she knew, and yet, she didn't. Couldn't. His mouth came down on hers and everything fell away but for what he could make her feel. Lacy's heart pounded like a drum. Her body ached; her mind swirled with the pleasure, the passion that she'd only ever found with Sam.

It was reaction, she told herself. That was all. It was the ache of her bones, the pain in her heart, finally being assuaged by the man who had caused it all in the first place.

He pulled her in tightly to him and for a brief, amazing moment, she allowed herself to feel the joy in being pressed against his hard, muscled chest again. To experience his arms wrap around her, enfolding her. To part her lips for his tongue and know the wild rush of sensation sweeping through her.

It was all there. Two years and all it took was a single kiss to remind her of everything they'd once shared, they'd once known. Her body leaned into him even as her mind was screaming at her to stop. She burned and in the flames, felt the heat sear every nerve ending. That was finally enough, after what felt like a small eternity, to make her listen to that small, rational internal voice.

Pulling away from him, Lacy shook her head and said, "No. No more. I won't do it."

"We just did."

Her head snapped up, furious with him, but more so with herself. How could she be so stupid? He'd *abandoned* her and he's back on the mountain for a single day and she's kissing him? God, it was humiliating. "That was a mistake."

"Not from where I'm standing," Sam said, but she was pleased to see he looked as shaken as she felt.

Small consolation, but she'd take it. The office suddenly seemed claustrophobic. She had to get out. Get into the open where she could think again, where she could force herself to remember all of the pain she'd been through because of him.

"You can't touch me again, Sam," Lacy said, and it cost her, because her body was still buzzing as if she'd brushed up against a live wire. "I won't let you."

Frowning, he asked, "Loyal to the new guy, huh?"

"No," she told him flatly, "this is about me. And about protecting myself."

"From *me*?" He actually looked astonished. "You really think you need protection from me?"

Could he really not understand this? "You once asked me to trust you. To believe that you loved me and you'd never leave."

His features went taut, his eyes shuttered. She *felt* him closing himself down, but she couldn't stop now.

"But you lied. You *did* leave."

His eyes flashed once—with hurt or shame, she didn't know, couldn't tell. "You think I planned to leave, Lacy? You think it was something I wanted?"

"How would I know?" she countered, anger and hurt clawing at her insides. "You didn't talk to me, Sam. You shut me out. And then you walked away. You hurt me once, Sam. I won't let you do it again. So you really need to back off."

"I'm here now, Lacy. And there's no way I'm backing off. This is still my home."

"But *I'm* not yours," she told him, accepting the pain of those words. "Not anymore."

He took a breath, blew it out and scrubbed one hand across the back of his neck. The familiarity of that gesture tugged at her.

"I thought of you," he admitted, fixing his gaze to hers as his voice dropped to a low throb that seemed to rumble along her spine. "I missed you."

Equal parts pleasure and pain tore at her heart. The taste of him was still on her mouth, flavoring every breath. Her senses were so full she felt as if she might explode. So she held tight to the pain and let the pleasure slide away. "It's your own fault you missed me, Sam. You're the one who left."

"I did what I had to do at the time."

"And screw anyone else," she added for him.

Pushing one hand through his hair, he finally took a step back, giving Lacy the breathing room she so badly needed. "That's what it looked like, I guess."

"That's what it was, Sam," she told him, and took the opportunity to slip out and move around until the desk once again stood between them like a solid barrier. "You left us all. Me. Your parents. Your sister. You walked away from your home and left the rest of us to pick up the pieces."

"I couldn't do it." He whirled around to face her, green eyes flashing like a forest burning. "You need to hear me say it? That I couldn't take it? That Jack died and I lost it? Fine. There." He slapped both hands onto the desk and glared at her. "That make it better for you? Easier?"

Overwhelmed with fury, Lacy thought she actually *saw* red. So many emotions surged inside her, she could hardly separate them. Lacy felt the crash and slam of the feelings she'd tried to bury two years ago as they rushed to the surface, demanding to be acknowledged.

"Better? Really?" Her voice was hard, but low. She wouldn't shout. Wouldn't give him the satisfaction of knowing just how deeply his words had cut her. "You think it can get better? My *husband* left me with all the casualness of tossing out an old shirt."

"I didn't—"

"Don't even try to argue," she interrupted him before he could.

"I won't." He fisted his hands on the desktop, then carefully, deliberately, released them again. "I can't explain it to myself, so how could I explain it to you or anyone else? Yeah, I left and maybe that was wrong."

"Maybe?"

"But I'm back now."

Lacy shook her head and swallowed the rest of her temper. Clashing with him was no way to prove to Sam that she was over him. She would *not* get pulled into a Wyatt family drama. She wasn't one of them anymore. Sam returning had nothing to do with her. In spite of the heat inside her, the yearning gnawing at her, she knew she had to protect herself.

"You didn't come back for me, Sam. So let's not pretend different, okay?"

"What if I had?" he whispered, gaze locked with hers.

"It wouldn't matter," she told him, and hoped to heaven he believed her. "What we had is done and gone."

He studied her for a long minute. Seconds ticked past, counting off with every heartbeat. Tension coiled and bristled in the air between them.

"I think," he said at last, "we just proved that what we had isn't completely gone."

"That doesn't count."

Surprised, he snorted, and laughter glinted in his eyes for a split second. "Oh, it counts. But we'll let it go for now."

She released a breath she hadn't realized she was holding. Ridiculous to feel both relieved and irritated all at once. How easily he turned what he was feeling on and off. How easily he had walked away from his life. From her.

"Back to business, then," he said, voice cool, dispassionate, as if that soul-shaking kiss hadn't happened. "Yesterday, you and Kristi were talking about the End of Season party."

"Yes. The plans are finalized."

Fine. Business she could do. She had been running the Wyatt resort for the past year and she'd done a damn good job. Let him go over the records and he would see for himself that she hadn't curled up and died just because he left. Lacy had a life she loved, a job she was good at. She was *happy*, damn it.

Coming around the desk, she ignored him and hit a few keys on the computer to pull up the file. "You can see for yourself, everything's in motion and right on schedule."

She moved out of the way as he stepped in to glance at the monitor. Scrolling down, he gave the figures there a quick look, then shifted his gaze to hers. "Looks fine. But end of season's usually not until March. Why are we closing the slopes early?"

Lacy was on familiar ground here and she relaxed a little as she explained, "There hasn't been any significant snowfall since early January. Weather's been cold enough to keep the snowpack in good shape, but we're getting icy now. Our guests expect the best powder in the world—"

"Yeah," he said wryly, "I know."

Of course he knew. He had, just like Lacy, grown up skiing the very slopes they were discussing now. He'd built a life, a profession, a reputation on skiing.

"Right. Then you should appreciate why we're doing the official closing early." Lacy walked around the desk until it stood between them again. She sighed and said, "Numbers have been falling off lately. People know there's no fresh snow, so they're not in a rush to come up the mountain.

"Throwing the End of Season party early will bring them up here. The hotel's already booked and we just have two of the cabins left empty…"

"One," he said, interrupting the flow of words while he continued to scan the plans for the party.

"One what?"

"One cabin's empty." He shrugged. "I moved my stuff into Cabin 6."

A sinking sensation opened up in the pit of her stomach. Cabin 6 was close to her house. Way too close. And he knew that. So had he chosen that cabin purposely? "I thought you'd be staying in the family quarters at the lodge."

He shook his head. "No. The cabin will suit me. I need the space."

"Fine," she said shortly, determined not to let it matter where he stayed. "Anyway, locals will still come ski whether we're 'officially' closed or not. We'll keep the lifts running and if we get more snow, then others will come, too. But holding the party early gives us publicity that could keep tourists coming in until the snow melts."

"It's a good idea."

He said it grudgingly and Lacy scowled at him. "You sound surprised."

"I'm not," he said, then dropped into the desk chair. "You know this place as well as I do. You were a good choice to run the resort. Why would I be surprised that you're good at your job?"

Was there a compliment in there?

"I want to go over the rest of the records, then, since you're the manager now, I'll want to talk tomorrow about the plans for the resort."

"Fine," she said, headed for the door. "I'll see you here tomorrow, then."

"That'll work."

She opened the door and stopped when he spoke again.

"And Lacy…"

She looked over her shoulder at him. His eyes met hers. "We're not done. We'll *never* be done."

There was nothing she could say to that, so she left, closing the door softly behind her.

That kiss stayed with him for hours.

For two years, he'd lived without her. It hadn't been easy, especially at first. But the grief and rage and guilt had colored everything then and he'd buried her memory in the swamp of other emotions. He'd convinced himself she was fine because the reality was too brutal. She'd come to haunt him at night of course. His sleep was crowded with her image, with her scent, with her taste.

And now he'd had a taste of her again and his system was on fire.

Need crouched inside him, clawing at his guts, tearing at what was left of his heart. He'd loved her back then. But love hadn't been enough to survive his own pain. Now there was desire, rich and thick and tormenting him in ways he hadn't felt since the last time he'd seen Lacy Sills.

She'd said she had a new man. Who the hell was touching her? Who heard her whisper of breath when she climaxed? Who felt her small, strong hands sliding up and down his skin? It was making Sam crazy just thinking about it. And yet, he couldn't seem to stop, either.

Yeah, none of it was rational. He didn't care.

When he'd headed home, his only thought had been for his father. Worry had driven every action. He hadn't stopped to think what it would be like to be near Lacy again. To face her and what he'd done by leaving. His heart told him he was a bastard, but his brain kept reminding him that he'd had to leave. That he might have made even more of a mess of things if he'd stayed.

Now he was here, for at least a few months. How was he going to make it without touching her? Answer— he wouldn't. The truth was, he was *going* to touch her. As soon and as often as possible. Her response to his kiss told him that whether she wanted to admit it or not, she wanted him, too. So to hell with the new guy, whoever he was.

Sam turned in the chair and looked out at the night. The lights glittering in the Salt Lake Valley below smudged the horizon with a glow that dimmed the stars. His gaze shifted, sweeping across the resort, where lights were golden, tossing puddled yellow illumination on the snow. It was pristine, beautiful, and he'd missed the place.

Acknowledging it was hard, but Sam knew that coming back here eased something inside him that had been drawn tight as a bowstring for two years. Coming home hadn't been easy. He'd spent the past two years trying to convince himself that he'd never come back. Now that he was here, though, there were ghosts to face, the past to confront and, mostly, there was the need to make a kind of peace with Lacy.

But then, he thought as he stood and walked out of the office, maybe it wasn't peace he was after with her.

For the next few days, Lacy avoided him at every turn and Sam let her get away with it. There was time to settle what was between them. He didn't have to rush, and besides, if he made her that nervous, drawing out the tension would only make her more on edge.

And that could only work to his benefit. Lacy cool and calm wasn't what he wanted. The temper she'd developed intrigued him and made him think of how passionate she had always been in bed. Together, they had been combustible. He wanted that back.

He glanced at her and almost smiled at the deliberate distance she kept. As if it would help. As if it could cool the fires burning between them. The day was cold and clear and the snow-covered ground at the summit crunched underfoot as they walked toward the site for the restaurant he was planning.

Tearing his gaze from Lacy momentarily, Sam studied the snack shop that had been there since before he was born. Small and filled with tradition, it had outlived its purpose. These days, most people wanted healthy food, not hot dogs smothered in mustard and chili.

"What're you thinking?" Lacy looked up at him, clearly still irritated that he'd dragged her away from the inn to come up here and look around.

He glanced at her. "That I want a chili dog."

For a split second, the ice in her eyes drained away. "You always did love Mike's chili."

"I've been all over the world and never found anything like it."

"Not surprising," Lacy answered. "I think he puts rocket fuel in that stuff."

Sam grinned and she gave him a smile in return that surprised and pleased him. A cold wind rushed across the mountaintop and lifted her blond braid off her shoulder. Her cheeks were pink, her blue eyes glittering and she looked so good it was all he could do not to grab her. But even as he thought it, her smile faded.

"I think we'll keep the snack shack for old time's sake," he said, forcing himself to look away from her and back out over the grounds where he would build the new restaurant. "But the new place, I'd like it to go over there," he pointed, "so the pines can ring the back of it. We'll have a deck out there, too, a garden area, and the trees will provide some shade, as well."

She looked where he pointed and nodded. "It's a good spot. But a wood deck requires a lot of upkeep. What about flagstone?"

Sam thought about it. "Good idea. Easier to clean, too. I called Dennis Barclay's construction company last night and he's going to come up tomorrow, make some measurements, draw up some plans so we can go to the city and line up the permits."

"Dennis does good work." She made a note on her iPad. "Franklin stone could lay the gravel paths and the flagstone. They've got a yard in Ogden with samples."

"Good idea. We can check that out once we get the permits and an architect's drawing on the restaurant."

"Right." Her voice was cool, clipped. "We used Nancy Frampton's firm for the addition to the inn."

"I remember." He nodded. "She's good. Okay, I'll call and talk to her tomorrow. Tell her what we want up here."

She made another note and he almost chuckled. She was so damn determined to keep him at arm's length. To pretend that what they'd shared in the office last night hadn't really happened. And he was willing to let that pretense go on. For a while.

"As long as you're making notes, write down that we want to get some ideas for where to build an addition to the inn. I want it close enough to the main lodge that it's still a part of us. But separate, too. Maybe joined by a covered walkway so even during storms, people can go back and forth."

"That'd work." She stopped, paused and said, "You know, a year ago, we put in a restaurant-grade stove, oven and fridge in the main lodge kitchen. We're equipped to provide more than breakfast and lunch now."

He turned his head and looked at her. "Then why aren't you?"

"We need a new chef." Lacy sighed and pulled her sunglasses off the top of her head to rest on the bridge of her nose. "Maria's ready to retire but she won't go until she's sure we'll survive without her."

Sam smiled, thinking of the woman who'd been at the lodge since he was a boy. Maria was a part of Sam's childhood, as much a fixture on the mountain as the Wyatt lodge itself. "Then she'll never leave."

Lacy smiled, too, and he wondered if she realized it. "Probably not. But if we want to serve a wider menu to more people, we need another chef to take some of the work off her shoulders. Maria doesn't really want to retire anyway, but she can't handle a larger load, no matter what she says. Another chef would make all the difference."

"Make a note," he said.

"Already done."

"Okay then." Sam took her elbow and turned her toward the snack bar. "Come on. We've got to go down and finalize the party setup. But first—chili dogs. On me."

"No thanks. I'm not hungry."

"As I remember it, you're always hungry, Lacy," he said, practically dragging her to the snack bar.

"Oh, for—" She broke off, gave in and started walking with him. "Things change, you know."

She was right. A lot had changed. But that buzz of something hot and electric that hummed between them was still there. Stronger than ever. Two years away hadn't eased what he felt for her. And since that kiss, he knew she felt the same.

"Mike's chili hasn't changed. And that's all I'm thinking about right now."

Of course, he was also planning ahead. So no onions.

Four

"Dad's really glad Sam's home." Kristi drained the last of her wine, then reached out and snagged the bottle off the coffee table for a refill.

"I know," Lacy said, sipping hers more slowly. She remembered the too-much-wine-and-brownies fest she and Kristi had had just a few days ago, and Lacy could live without another morning-after headache. "Your mom's happy, too."

Kristi sighed and snuggled deeper into the faded, overstuffed chair opposite Lacy. "I know. She hasn't stopped baking. Pies, cakes, the cookies I brought over to share. It's nuts, really. I don't think the oven's cooled off once since Sam arrived. Between Mom's sugar overload and Maria making all of Sam's favorites for dinner...I think I've gained five pounds."

While her best friend talked, Lacy stared at the fire in the brick hearth. Outside, the night was cold and still, moonlight glittering on snow. Inside, there was warmth from the fire and from the deep threads of friendship.

It felt good to sit here relaxing—or as much as she could relax when the conversation was about Sam. But at least he wasn't *here*. He wasn't walking through the resort with her, hunched over her desk going over plans, smelling so good she wanted to crawl onto his lap, tuck her head against his chest and just breathe him in.

Oh, God.

It had been days now and her very righteous anger kept sliding away to dissolve in a puddle of want and need. She didn't *want* to want Sam, but it seemed there was no choice. And damn it, Lacy told herself, she should know better.

What they had together hadn't been enough to keep him with her two years ago. It wouldn't be enough now. Wanting him was something she couldn't help. That didn't mean that she would surrender to what she felt for him again, though.

"They're all so happy he's back," Kristi was saying. "It's like they've forgotten all about how he left."

"I can understand that," Lacy told her, pausing for another sip of wine to ease the dryness in her suddenly tight throat. It was different for his family, of course. Having Sam back meant filling holes in their lives that had stood empty for too long. There was no second-guessing what they felt at his return. They weren't focused on their pain now, but on the alleviation of it.

Taking a breath, Lacy gave her friend a smile she really didn't feel. "Your parents missed him horribly. They're just grateful to have him home."

"Yeah, I get it." Kristi frowned into her straw-colored wine. "But how do they just ignore how he left? What he did to all of us by leaving *when* he did?"

"I don't know." Lacy reached out to snag a chocolate chip cookie off the plate on the table. Taking a bite, she chewed thoughtfully while Kristi continued to rant about her older brother, then she said, "I think for your mom and dad, it's more about getting their son back than it is punishing him for leaving."

"He hurt us all."

"Yeah. He did." Lacy knew how the other woman felt. *She* couldn't get past how Sam had left, either. Having him here now was so hard. Every time she saw him. Every time he stepped close to her, her heartbeat staggered and the bottom dropped out of her stomach.

Plus, there was the whole kiss thing, too. She hadn't been able to forget it. Hadn't been able to stop thinking about it. Had spent the past several days on red alert, waiting for him to try it again so she could shut him down flat.

And he hadn't tried.

Damn it.

"I used to think," Kristi said softly, "that everything would be better if Sam just came home." She paused for a sip of wine. "Now he has and it's not better. It's just… I don't know."

"He's your brother, Kristi," Lacy said, propping her feet on the coffee table and crossing them at the ankles. "You're still mad at him, but you love him and you know you're glad he's back."

"Do you?"

"Do I what?"

"Still love him."

Lacy's heart gave a hard thump. "That's not the point."

"It's completely pointy."

"Funny." Lacy took a long drink of her wine and

when she'd swallowed, said, "But this isn't about me. Or what I feel."

"So," Kristi mused, a half smile on her face, "that's a yes."

"No, it's not." Because her heart hammered every time he was near didn't necessarily mean *love*. Desire would always be there and that she could accept. Love was something else again and, "Even if it was, it wouldn't matter."

"You're still mad, too."

Lacy sighed. "Yeah. I am."

"He's worked really hard on the End of Season party," Kristi grudgingly admitted. "Sam even called one of his old friends. Tom Summer? He has a band that's really popular now and Sam talked Tom into bringing the band in for the party. Live music's going to be way better than the stereo we had arranged."

"Yes, it will." Irritating to admit that Sam had so easily arranged for a good band when everyone Lacy had spoken to about playing at the party had already been booked. He had friends everywhere and they were all as pleased to have him back as his family was. Here at Snow Vista, it was a regular *Celebration of Sam*. And Lacy was the only one not playing along. Well, okay, there was Kristi, as well. But she would eventually join the parade—Sam was her brother and that connection would win in the end.

When that happened, Lacy would be off by herself. Standing on the sidelines. Alone.

"It's like he's stepped right back into his life without a miss." Kristi shook her head again. "He steers away from most of the skiers—I think that's because everyone wants to ask him about Jack and he doesn't want to talk about him. I can't blame Sam for that." Her index finger ringed the rim of her wineglass. "None of us do."

"True." Lacy herself had seen Sam keep away from strangers, from the tourists who flocked to ski at Snow Vista. Just as she had watched him visit all of the runs on the mountain but the one that Jack had favored. She knew that memories were choking him just as her own had for two years.

Even this cabin—where she had grown up—wasn't a sanctuary anymore. Instead of memories of days spent with her father, the images in her mind were all of her and Sam, starting their life together. Lacy glanced around the familiar room, seeing the faded but comfortable furniture, the brightly colored throw rugs, the photos and framed prints hanging on the wall.

When she and Sam had married, they'd moved into her place—the plan had been to stay there and add on to the simple cabin until they had their dream house. The cabin was in a perfect spot—great views, close to the lodge and the ski runs—plus it was hers, free and clear, left to her after her father's death. Of course, those building plans were gathering dust in a closet and the rooms for the children they'd planned to have had never been built.

But staying here in this cabin had been a sort of exquisite torture. She'd heard Sam's voice, felt his presence, long after he left. Even her bed felt too big without him sharing it with her. Sam had torn up the foundation of her life and left her sitting in the rubble.

"Sam's even talking to Dad about building a summer luge ride. One like Park City has, to give tourists something to do up here in summer." Frowning, she took a sip of wine and grumbled, "I hate that it's a good idea."

"I know what you mean," Lacy admitted, chewing

on another cookie. "I want him to be out of step, you know? To stumble a little when he takes charge after two years gone. And yet, he's doing it all and he's getting a lot done. He's already had a contractor up at the summit to see about building the new restaurant and he's hired Nancy Frampton to draw up plans." She took a huge bite of the cookie and ground her teeth together. "He's gotten more done in the last few days than we have in two years."

"Irritating as hell, isn't it?" Kristi muttered.

"Really is."

"I don't know if I want him here or not. I mean, I'm glad for Mom and Dad—they missed him so much. But seeing him every day..." She stopped, her eyes widened and she groaned out loud. "God, I'm spewing all over the place and this has got to be so much worse on you." Instantly, Kristi looked contrite, embarrassed. "How are you handling it?"

"I'm fine." Lacy figured if she said those two words often enough, they might actually click in and she'd *be* fine.

At the moment, though, not so much. Her gaze shifted to the closest window. Through it, she had a view of the snow-covered forest, a wide sweep of sky, and there, she thought, through the trees, a glimpse of Cabin 6.

Most of the time she could pretend he wasn't there, but at night, when he had the lights on, he was impossible to ignore. As she watched, she saw his shadow pass a window and her heartbeat fluttered. Having him that close was a new kind of torture, she told herself.

For two years, she hadn't known where he was or what he was doing, except for the occasional updates from his parents or snippets in the media. Being apart from him tore at her—at least in the first few months. Now he was here, and still out of reach—not that she wanted to reach out and touch him. But having him close by and yet separate was harder than she'd imagined it could be.

When he first told her he'd be staying in the cabin closest to her home, Lacy had worried that he'd be coming over. But not once had Sam walked to her door. And she didn't know if that made her feel better or worse. The only thing she was sure of was that her nerves were stretched taut and sooner or later, they were going to snap.

"You're not fine." Kristi's voice was soft and filled with understanding.

Lacy might have argued that point, but Kristi was her best friend. They'd seen each other through high school, college courses, mean girls and heartbreak. What would be the point of trying to hold out now?

"Okay, no, I'm not." Nodding, Lacy held her wineglass a little tighter and drew a long, deep breath. "But I can be. It's just going to take some time."

"I hate that you're getting all twisted up by him again."

"Thanks," Lacy said, forcing a smile. "Me, too."

"The problem is, we're letting him get to us," Kristi said, grabbing another cookie and taking a bite. "That gives him all the power. What we have to do is take it back."

"You've been reading self-help books again." Lacy shook her head.

A quick grin flashed over Kristi's face. "Guilty. But you know, some of what they say makes sense. He can only bug us if we allow it. So we just have to stop allowing it."

"What a great idea," Lacy said, laughing, and God it felt good to laugh. "Got any ideas on how?"

Kristi shrugged. "Haven't gotten to that chapter yet."

"How does Tony maintain sanity around you?"

Tony DeLeon was smart, gorgeous and hopelessly in love with Kristi. For the past year or so, they'd been inseparable and Lacy really tried to be happy for her friend and not envious.

"He loves me." Kristi sighed dreamily. "Who would have guessed that I'd fall for an accountant?"

"Good thing you did—he's done a great job handling the inn's books."

"Yeah, he's pretty amazing," Kristi mused. "And so not the issue here. The problem is Sam."

Lacy's problem had always been Sam. She'd known from the time she was fifteen that he was the one she wanted. Oh, Jack was what the newspapers had always called "the fun twin" and she supposed that was true. Sam was quieter. More intense. Jack had been larger than life. His laugh was loud and booming; his love for life had been huge.

And when he died, he'd taken pieces of everyone who loved him with him. The largest piece had come from Sam. Those had been dark, terrible days. Lacy had helplessly watched Sam sink into a pit of misery and grief. Even lying beside him in their bed here at the cabin, she'd felt him slipping away from her.

He'd gotten lost, somehow, in the pain and he hadn't been able to find his way out.

But knowing that didn't make what had happened between them any easier to bear.

"Kristi," she said, "he's your brother. You can't stay mad at him forever."

Unexpectedly Kristi's eyes filled with tears, but she

blinked them back. "We *all* lost Jack and Sam didn't seem to understand that. He hurt me. Hurt all of us. Are we just supposed to forgive and forget?"

"I don't know," Lacy said, though she knew that she would never forget that she'd been left behind. Shut out. Made to feel that she didn't matter. She'd lived through that as a child and she'd trusted Sam when he promised he would never leave her—then he did, and that pain would never completely disappear.

"I don't think I can," Kristi admitted. She set her wineglass on the table and stood up. Then she walked to a window and stared out at the lamplight streaming from Sam's cabin. "I want to," she said, sending a short glance over her shoulder at Lacy. "I really do. And Tony keeps telling me that I'm only hurting myself by hanging on to all of this anger..."

Smiling, Lacy asked, "Gave him one of your books to read, did you?"

A soft, sad chuckle shot from Kristi's throat. "Yeah, guess I'm going to have to stop that." She turned her back on the window and shrugged. "It shouldn't be this hard."

No, it shouldn't.

"You'll just have to keep trying," Lacy told her.

"What about you?" her friend asked quietly. "Are you going to try?"

"My situation's different, Kristi. He's your family." Lacy stood up and cleared the coffee table of the cookies and wine. It had been a long day and clearly this girlfest was winding down into a pit of melancholy. She'd rather take a hot bath and go to bed. Straightening, she looked at the woman watching her. "He was my family, now he's not. So it doesn't really matter what I think of him."

Kristi gave her a sad smile. "Of course it matters. *You* matter, Lacy. I don't want him to hurt you again."

Winking, Lacy deliberately brought up Kristi's self-help advice. "He can only hurt me if I *allow* it. And trust me, I won't."

The party was a huge success. It was still early in the evening and Snow Vista was packed with locals and tourists who were enjoying the clear, cold weather and the hum of energy. The crowds were thick; music pumped into the air with a pounding beat that seemed to reverberate up from the ground. All around Sam, people were talking, laughing, dancing. The party was a success. So why the hell was he so on edge?

Then he realized why.

It had been two years since he'd been in a crowd this size. He'd avoided mobs of people like the plague. It was always Jack who'd enjoyed the adoring masses. Sam's twin had fed off the admiration and applause. He'd loved being the center of attention, always making his ski runs faster, his jumps higher, his freestyle twists riskier.

All to push the edges of an envelope that never had a chance to hold him. Jack was the adventurer, Sam thought, a half smile curving his mouth as he remembered. Even as kids, Jack would go off the beaten path, skiing between trees, jumping over rocks, and once he'd even gone over a cliff edge and landed himself in a thigh-high cast for eight weeks.

Basically, Jack had loved the rush of speed. If he hadn't, maybe he wouldn't have died in a fiery car wreck. So useless. Such a waste. And so like Jack to drive himself to his own limits and beyond. He hadn't considered risks. Hadn't worried about consequences.

It was almost as if he'd come into his life hungry for every experience he could find. There was a time Sam had admired—envied—Jack's ability to cruise through the world getting exactly what he wanted out of it.

Jack had loved the publicity, the reporters, seeing himself on the glossy pages of magazines. Adulation had been his drug of choice.

"Hell," Sam muttered, "this party would have been a showcase for Jack. He'd have been right in the center of it all, holding court, laughing." Shoving his hands into his jeans pockets, Sam glanced at the black sky overhead. "Damned if I don't miss you."

"Mr. Wyatt!"

Sam's head swiveled and he spotted a slim blonde woman with short hair clutching a microphone, headed right at him. Worse, there was a cameraman hot on her heels.

A reporter.

Everything in him tightened, like fists ready for battle. There was a time when Sam had handled the media like a pro. When he was skiing, competing, he was used to being in front of a camera and answering what always seemed like moronic questions. But then Jack died and the questions had changed and ever since, Sam had dodged as many reporters as he could.

That wasn't an option tonight, though, and he knew it. The End of Season party was big news around here, and as Lacy had pointed out, the more publicity they got, the better it was for Snow Vista's bottom line.

So he gritted his teeth, planted his feet wide apart in a fighting stance and waited.

"Mr. Wyatt," the woman said again as she got closer. She gave him a fabulous smile, then turned and looked at her cameraman. "Scott, just set up right here. We'll get the party in the background for atmosphere."

She hadn't even asked if he'd speak to her. Just assumed he would. The reporter was probably used to most people wanting to do anything to get on camera for a few minutes.

When the light flashed on, Sam squinted briefly, then looked to the woman. Around him, the curious began to gather, with the occasional teenager making faces and waving to the camera.

"I'm Megan Short reporting for Channel Five," the woman said, her smile fake, her voice sharp and clipped. "I'd like to talk to you about this event, if you've got a few minutes."

"Sure," he said with what he hoped was more enthusiasm than he felt.

"Great." She turned, faced the camera and, when the guy behind the lens gave her a signal, she started right in. "This is Megan Short and I'm reporting from Snow Vista resort where the annual End of Season party is under way."

Sam forced himself to relax, taking a deep breath. While he half listened to the reporter, he let his gaze slide over the raucous crowd. More gathered behind him, jostling to get on camera, but most were too busy partying to pay attention. The music still pounded, people were laughing, kids were ice-skating on the pond. The air was cold and the sky was clear. A perfect night really—but for the reporter.

"In recent years, the party at Snow Vista just hasn't been the same, some residents have claimed," Megan was saying as she turned from the camera to look up at Sam. "But tonight, it looks like everything is as it should be. And I think that's due to the return of local champion Sam Wyatt." She turned, gave him another fatuous smile and continued, "What's it like for you, Sam, to be back here where you and your twin, Jack, once ruled the slopes?"

He sucked in a gulp of frosty air and pushed it forcefully into his lungs. *Of course she would bring up Jack. Tragedy made for great TV, after all.*

"It's good to be home." He hoped she let it go at that, but he knew she wouldn't.

"Your brother's tragic death two years ago left the entire state reeling," she was saying, with a thread of insincere sympathy coloring the words. "We were all invested in the success of the Wyatt twins. How does it feel, Sam, to be here without Jack?"

Under the building rage ran a slender thread of helpless frustration. Why did reporters always ask *how does it feel*? Could they really not guess? Or did they not care that they were digging into open wounds and dumping handfuls of salt into them? He had a feeling it was a little of both along with the hope of getting an emotional reaction out of their victims—and if there were tears, that was a bonus.

Well she wouldn't get what she wanted from him. He had plenty of experience dealing with those who sought to pry into feelings best left alone. His features shuttered as he locked away emotions and buried them deep.

"Jack loved the End of Season party," he said, keeping his voice even and steady, though the effort cost him. "So it's good to be here, watching locals and visitors alike enjoy the festivities."

"I'm sure, but—"

He cut her off and pretended not to see the flash of anger in her eyes. "Tom Summer's band is great. If you'll swing your camera around, you'll see we've got the kiddie pond open for ice-skating and there are more than two dozen food booths set up offering everything from pizza to Korean barbecue to funnel cakes." He smiled into the camera and ignored the sputtering reporter beside him.

"Yes," she said, determined to steer him back on the course she'd chosen. "And yet, how much more special would it be for you to be here tonight if your twin hadn't died so tragically? Is that loss still resonating within the Wyatt family?"

He'd tried, Sam assured himself. He'd put on a good face, pushed the resort and made an effort to ignore the woman's painful digging. But there was only so much a man could take. Damned if he'd let this woman feed off his family's pain. He sent her a steely-eyed glare that had her backing up one small step. But the determination in her eyes didn't dim.

"No comment," he said tightly even though he realized that a statement as simple as that one to a reporter was like waving a red flag at a bull.

"The loss of a twin has to be difficult to deal with—"

"Difficult?" Such a small, weak word to describe what Jack's loss had done to him. To the family. "I think this interview is finished."

She was relentless. Obviously, she'd set a goal for herself and had no intention of walking away until she'd succeeded in her mission.

"I can't imagine what it must have been like for you," she was saying, moving in closer so that she and Sam shared the same camera frame. "Competing with your twin, then becoming a bone-marrow donor during his battle with leukemia…"

Sam kept breathing—that was all he could do. If he spoke now, it wouldn't be pretty. It all rushed back at him. The stunning news that Jack had cancer. The treat-ments. Watching his strong, fit brother weaken under the stress of the chemo. And finally, Sam, donating his bone marrow in a last-ditch attempt to save the other half of himself.

The transplant worked. And over the span of several weeks, Jack's strength returned. His powerful will and resolve to reclaim his life drove him to recover, become the man he used to be.

Just in time to die.

"…helping him win that battle," the reporter was say-ing, "defeat cancer only to die in an horrific car accident on his way to the airport to compete in the international ski trials." She pushed the microphone up higher. "Tell us," she urged, "in your own words, what it cost you and your family to survive such a personal tragedy."

His brain was buzzing. His heartbeat thundered in his own ears. His mouth was dry and once again, he clenched his hands into useless fists. Sam gritted his teeth because he knew, if he opened his mouth to speak, he was going to blast the woman for her feigned sym-pathy in the name of ratings.

"Megan Short!" Lacy stepped up beside Sam, smiled at the reporter and said, "This is great! I'm Lacy Sills, manager of the resort. We're so happy to have Chan-nel Five at Snow Vista. I hope everyone in your audi-ence will come on up to join the party! We've got free food, a skating rink for the kids, dancing to a live band and the best desserts in Utah. The evening's young so come up and join us!"

Undeterred, Megan shifted her attention to Lacy. "Thank you, Lacy, for that invitation. Maybe you could answer my question, though. Our viewers watched Sam and Jack Wyatt over the years, as the twins scooped up pretty much every available prize and award available for skiing. Now, since you were once married to Sam, maybe you could share with our viewers just how hard it is for you to deal not only with the ghost of Jack Wyatt, but with your own ex-husband."

For a split second, Sam had been torn when Lacy hurried up. Glad to see her, but irritated that she'd obviously believed he needed rescuing. What was most surprising, though, was that she would come to his aid in the first place. He'd been home nearly a week and she'd done everything she could to avoid him. Now she rushed in? Why?

He looked at her, wearing a navy blue sweater, jeans and boots, her thick blond braid hanging over one shoulder. No one else would have noticed, but Sam could see what it cost Lacy to stand there and smile at the woman taunting her.

Lacy's chin lifted, her eyes flashed and Sam felt a swell of pride. When she met the reporter's gaze, he remembered all of the times over the years when Lacy had stood her ground in spite of everything. Damn, she was something to see. Admiration and desire twisted together inside him.

"I really can't talk about Jack Wyatt other than to say we all miss him. Always will." Face frozen into a tight smile, Lacy added, "Thanks so much for coming to the resort tonight and I hope all of your viewers will come up the mountain to enjoy the End of Season party! Now, if you'll excuse us, Sam and I have a few things to take care of..."

Not waiting for an assent, Lacy threaded her arm through Sam's and tugged. He took the escape she offered. Leading her away from the crowds, Sam stalked around the peripheries of the noisy mob until they were far enough away from everyone that he felt he could draw an easy breath again. They stood in the shadows behind the main lodge. Here, the music was distanced and so were the shouts and conversations and laughter.

If Lacy hadn't shown up when she did, Sam thought he might have told that reporter exactly what he thought of her. And that wouldn't have been good for him or the resort. "Thanks," he said when he could unclench his teeth enough for words to sneak past.

"No problem," she assured him, and leaned against the building. "I've been dealing with Megan Short for the last two years. She's relentless."

"Like a damn shark," he muttered, shoving one hand through his hair, furious that he'd allowed the woman to get to him.

"Please," Lacy said on a snort of laughter. "She makes sharks look like fluffy kittens. Everyone she interviews on camera either ends up crying or screaming at her or threatening her."

"You handled her."

She shrugged.

"What I'm wondering is why," he said. "You could have left me swinging in the wind and didn't. So... why?"

Lacy pushed away from the wall. "I saw the look on your face. Another minute or two alone with her and you'd have ruined all the good publicity we're getting."

"That's it? For the good of the resort?"

She tipped her head back to look up at him. "Why else, Sam?"

"That's what I want to know." His gaze moved over her, sweeping up and down before settling finally on her eyes. "See, I think there's more to it than that. I think you still feel something."

She snorted. "I feel plenty. Just not for you."

A grin curved his mouth as Sam watched her fiddle with the end of her braid. She'd always done that when she was skirting the truth. "You're playing with your hair and we both know what that means."

Instantly, she stopped, tossed her braid behind her back and glared at him. "You know, here in the real world, when someone helps you out, you just say 'thanks.'"

"Already said thanks."

"Right. You did. You're welcome."

She turned to go and he stopped her with one hand on her arm. "We're not done."

Then he kissed her.

Five

Lacy should have pushed him away.

Should have kicked him, stomped on his foot, *something.*

Instead, she kissed him back.

How could she not? Two years of hungering for him made her just crazy enough to want his arms around her again. To feel his mouth on hers. His breath on her cheek.

For a heart-stopping moment, there was just the heat of him, holding her, tasting her. The erotic slide of his tongue against hers sent sparks of awareness dazzling through her body like tiny flames, awakening and dying and starting up again.

She leaned into him, the sound of the party nothing more than a buzz in her ears. How could she hear more, when her own heartbeat was crashing so loudly it drowned out everything else?

The black leather jacket he wore felt cold and slick

beneath her hands as she clung to his shoulders. Reaching up, she threaded her fingers through his hair, holding his mouth to hers, reveling in the sensations rushing inside.

He moved her backward until she was pressed against the back wall of the inn. The thick, cold logs sent chills down her spine even as the heat Sam engendered swamped them both. Years fell back, pain slipped away and all she was left with was the amazing sensations she'd only experienced with Sam. Anger fell beneath layers of passion and she *knew* it would be back, stronger than ever. Anger at him. At herself.

But right at the moment, she didn't care.

It was crazy. A party attended by crowds of people was going on not a hundred yards from them. They were out in the open, where anyone could stumble across them. And yet, all she could think was, *yes. More.*

His hands slid beneath the hem of her sweater to stroke across her abdomen and the chill of his touch warred with the heat—and lost. Lacy pushed herself into him, moving as close as she could and still it wasn't enough to feed the raw need pulsing within.

He tore his mouth from hers and they stared at each other, breaths coming fast and harsh, clouds of vapor pushing into the air between them. His gaze moved over her face. His eyes were shadowed in the dim light and still they seemed to shine a brilliant green.

A moment later, raucous laughter and a girl's flirty squeal shattered the spell holding them in a silent grip. Sam stepped back from her with a muttered curse just as a young couple ran around the side of the inn.

They came to a sliding stop on the snowy path. "Oh hey, man. Sorry. We were just looking…um…"

Clearly the young couple had been looking for the same privacy she and Sam were just enjoying.

Sam stuffed both hands into his jeans pockets. "It's fine. Enjoy the party."

"Yeah," the boy said and shot his girlfriend a quick grin. "We are."

They left as quickly as they'd appeared.

"Well, that was embarrassing." Lacy blew out a long breath, straightened her sweater and stepped back from Sam so she wouldn't be tempted to leap at him again.

"Lousy timing," he mumbled, his gaze locked on her.

"I think it was pretty good timing," she said, though her body disagreed. Another minute or two of Sam's kisses and she might have forgotten everything. Might have just given in to the need still clamoring inside her. Oh, there was no *might* about it, she admitted silently.

She'd wanted to be touched, kissed, loved. She'd wanted Sam as she had always wanted him. Knowing better didn't seem to help. Lacy had nearly drowned in the sea of her own anger and misery when Sam first left. To survive, she'd clawed her way out then closed and locked the door on those feelings, good and bad. She had had to forget—or at least try to forget, just how much she loved Sam.

Life would be a lot easier right now, she thought, if she'd only been able to hold on to that anger. Instead, it was the heat of lost love she felt, not the ice of pain.

"Lacy..."

"Don't," she said, holding up one hand and shaking her head. Talking to him was almost as dangerous to her as kissing him. His voice alone was a kind of music to her, that seemed to seep into her heart and soul whether she wanted it to or not. "Just...don't say anything."

"I want you."

"Damn it," she snapped, walking now, with long strides, moving toward the light and sound of the party, "I asked you not to say anything." Especially *that*.

"Not saying it doesn't change anything." He followed her, his much longer legs outpacing hers easily.

She whipped her head up to look at him. "This was a kiss, Sam. Just a kiss." It had been more and she knew it but damned if she'd admit it to him. Heck, she wasn't entirely comfortable admitting it to herself. "We were both strung a little tight and the tension snapped. That's *all*."

If that were true, she told herself, she'd be feeling a heck of a lot better right now. Instead, she was wound tighter than ever. It was a wonder her body wasn't throwing off sparks with every slam of her heartbeat.

He moved closer and Lacy held her ground. Probably dumb, but she wasn't going to give him the satisfaction of thinking that she couldn't handle being near him. Especially since she couldn't.

"If those kids hadn't come crashing around the corner, we'd still be having at each other."

"Call it fate," she said with a shrug that belied the tension still coursing through her. "Someone somewhere knows that this shouldn't have happened and they were cutting us a break."

"Or trying to kill me," he said, and one corner of his mouth lifted, though there wasn't a sign of humor in his eyes.

"The easy answer is," she pointed out, "keep your lips to yourself."

"I never did 'easy.' You should know that."

"Not fair," she said, shaking her head and giving him a hard look. "You don't get to do the 'remember when' thing with me, Sam." She backed up a step for good measure, but when he followed that move, she didn't bother backing up farther.

"It's our past, Lacy," he reminded her, his voice dropping to a low, sexy rumble.

"*Past* being the operative word." Lacy sighed and told herself to gather up the wispy threads of what had once been her self-control. "There's nothing between us anymore, so you shouldn't have kissed me again."

"Wasn't just me," he reminded her, and a cold wind whipped around the edge of the building and lifted his dark hair. "Won't be just me when it happens next time, either."

The band finished one song and the pause between it and the next hung in the sudden stillness. When the pounding beat of the drums kicked in once more, Lacy forced herself to say, "It won't happen."

"You said that the last time and yet, here we are."

She had said it. At the time, she had meant it, too. Lacy didn't want to get drawn back into the still-smoldering feelings she had for Sam. Didn't want to put herself through another agonizing heartbreak. It was just a damn shame that her body didn't have the same resolve as her mind.

"Why are you kissing me at all, Sam?" She asked the question again because she still didn't have an answer. "Why do you even want to? *You* left *me*, remember? You walked away from us and never gave me another thought. Why pretend now that this is anything more than raging hormones with nowhere else to go?"

He looked at her, but didn't speak. But then, what could he say?

With her words hanging in the cold, clear air, Lacy turned and walked hurriedly back to the safety of the crowd, losing herself in the mob of people.

* * *

By midnight, the party was over. Everyone had gone home or to their hotel rooms and the mountain was quiet again. The Snow Vista crew had taken care of cleanup, so all that was left to clear out in the morning were the booths that would have to be disassembled and stored until the next time they were needed.

The mountain was dark, but for the sprinkling of lamplight shining through windows at the main lodge and surrounding cabins. The sky was black and starlit, leaving a peaceful, serene night.

In contrast, Sam felt like a damned caged tiger. He couldn't settle. Couldn't relax. Just like he couldn't get Lacy out of his mind. She remained there, a shadow on his thoughts, even when he knew he shouldn't be thinking of her at all. Even when he knew it might be easier for all of them if he just did as she asked and left her alone.

But hell. Easier wasn't always what it was cracked up to be. He'd grown up skiing the fastest, most danger-ous runs he could find. Memories crowded his mind. But they weren't of skiing. They weren't of him and his twin, Jack, chasing danger all over the mountain. These memories were all Lacy. Her kiss. Her touch. The way she laughed one night when they'd walked through a snowstorm, tipping her head back and letting the fat flakes caress her cheeks. The shine in her hair, the warmth of her skin. All the things that had haunted him for the past two years.

Every moment with her stood out in his mind with glaring clarity and he knew he wouldn't be able to stay away from her.

Leaning against the doorjamb of his cabin, he looked through the woods toward Lacy's place. What had once been *their* place. There were lights in the windows and smoke curling lazily from the chimney.

His guts fisted. This was the hardest part of being home. Facing his family had been tough but being close to Lacy and not *with* her was torture. Leaving her had torn him up, coming home was harder still. A couple of kisses had only fed the banked fires inside him, and yet, all he wanted was another one.

"No," he muttered, one hand tightening on the wood door frame. "You want more than that. Much more."

He thought back over the past several days and realized that beneath the lust was a layer of annoyance. The Lacy he had left behind two years ago had been cool, calm. And crazy about him.

Sam could privately admit that he'd half expected her to jump into his arms with a cry of joy when he came back. And the fact that she hadn't, stung. Not only that, he had thought he'd be dealing with cool dispassion from her. Instead, there had been temper. Fury. Which, he had to say, was arousing. He liked that flash of anger in her eyes. Liked the heat that spilled off her whenever they were together. And he knew Lacy liked it, too.

She could argue all she wanted, fight what lay simmering between them, but the truth was, she still felt it, whether she wanted to or not.

Those kisses proved him right on that score.

Now his skin felt too tight. There was an itch inside him—damned if he'd ignore it any longer. This all began and ended with Lacy, he told himself. When he left Snow Vista two years before, he'd been wrapped up in his own grief and fury. Losing his twin had sliced at Sam's soul to the point where even breathing had seemed an insurmountable task. He'd deliberately exiled himself from this place. From her.

He'd picked up Jack's dreams and carried them for his dead twin—believing that he owed it to his brother. But dreams were damned empty when they weren't your own. Now Sam was back. To stay? He didn't know. But while he was here, he and Lacy were going to straighten out a few things.

Behind him, the heat of the room swelled, while in front of him, the cold and the dark beckoned. And he knew that whatever was between him and Lacy, it was time they settled it. He reached back to snatch his jacket off a hook. He was shrugging it on as he stepped into the night and closed the door behind him.

It didn't take him long to cross the distance separating his cabin from hers. And in those few moments, Sam asked himself why the hell he was doing this. But the simple fact was, he had to see her again. Had to get beyond the wall she had erected between them.

Stars were out and a pale half-moon lit the path, though he didn't need it. He could have found his way to Lacy's place blindfolded. On her wide front porch, he looked through the windows and saw a fire in the hearth, a couple of lamps tossing golden puddles across a hardwood floor. And he saw Lacy, curled up in a chair, staring at the flames as flickering shadow and light dazzled over her.

Even now, his heart gave a hard lurch and his body went like stone—but then, passion had never been a problem between them. He knocked on the door and watched as she frowned, pushed to her feet and walked to it.

She opened the door and her features went stiff. "Go away."

"No."

Lacy huffed out a breath. "What do you want?"

"To talk."

"No, thank you." She tried to close the door, but he slapped one hand to it and held it open.

He stepped past her and walked into the main room, ignoring her sputter of outrage. "You should close that door before you freeze."

Glaring at him, she looked as though she might argue the point, even though all she wore was a flannel sleep shirt, scooped at the neck, high on her thighs. Her long, toned legs were bare and the color of fresh cream. Her feet were bare, too, and he noted the sinful red polish on the nails. Her blond hair was free of its braid, hanging in heavy waves around her shoulders, making him want nothing more than to fist his hands in that thick, soft mass again. But her blue eyes were narrowed and there was no welcome there.

Finally, though, the winter cold was enough to convince her to shut the door, sealing the two of them in together. Still, she didn't cross the room, but stayed at the door, her back braced against it, her arms folded across her chest. "You don't have the right to come here. I didn't invite you."

"Didn't used to need an invitation."

Her mouth worked as if she were biting back words struggling to escape. The flannel nightshirt she wore shouldn't have been sexy, but it really was. Everything about this woman got to him as no one else ever had. He had thought he could walk away from her, but the truth was, he'd taken her with him everywhere he went.

"What do you want?"

"You know the answer to that." He shrugged out of his jacket and tossed it on the back of the nearest chair.

"Don't get comfortable. You won't be here that long."

One dark eyebrow lifted. "You don't want me to go, Lacy, and we both know it."

Frowning, she stared at him. "Sometimes we want things that aren't good for us."

"Been reading Kristi's self-help books?"

A brief smile curved her mouth and was gone again in an instant.

The wind whistled under the eaves and sounded like a breathless moan. The fire in the hearth jumped and hissed as that wind passed over the chimney and the golden light in the room swayed as if it was dancing.

"You left once. Why can't you just stay away?" she whispered.

"Because I can't get you out of my head."

She looked at him. "Try harder."

Sam laughed shortly, shook his head and moved toward her. "Won't do any good. Been trying for two years."

Those memories, images of her, were so ingrained inside him, Sam had about convinced himself that the reality of her couldn't possibly be as good as he remembered. And maybe that's why he was here now. To prove to himself, one way or another, what exactly it was that burned between him and Lacy.

"Sam…" She sighed and shook her head, as if denying what he was saying, what the two of them were feeling.

"Damn it Lacy, I want you. Never stopped wanting you." He moved in close enough to touch her and then stopped. He took a breath, drawing her scent deep inside.

Silence crowded down around them, the only sound the hiss and crackle of the flames in the hearth. His heart pounding, Sam waited for what felt like an eternity, until she finally lifted her eyes to his and said simply, "Me, too."

In a blink, Sam reached for her and she came into his arms as if they'd never been apart. He fisted his hands in the back of her soft, flannel gown and held her tight, pressing her length against him until he felt her heart thundering in time with his own. Bending his head, he took her mouth in a kiss that was both liberation and surrender.

Fires leaped within, burning him from the inside out and it was still only a flicker of the heat he felt just holding her. His tongue tangled with hers in a desperate dance of need. She gave herself up to the moment, leaning into him, running her hands up and down his arms until the friction of his own shirt against his skin added a new layer of torture.

Lost in the blinding passion spinning out of control, Sam reached down for the hem of her gown and in one quick yank, pulled it over her head and off. Lacy's blond hair spilled across her bare shoulders and lay like silk over his hands. His first look at her in two long years hit him hard. She was even more beautiful than he'd remembered and he couldn't wait another second to get his hands on her. He tossed the nightgown to the chair beside him and then covered her breasts with his palms.

She sighed, letting her head fall back as a murmured groan of pleasure slid from her throat. His thumbs and fingers stroked and rubbed her hardened nipples and he watched those summer-blue eyes of hers roll back as sensations took her over.

Burying his own groan, Sam's gaze swept up and down her body briefly before he shifted his hold on her, catching her at the waist and lifting her up so he could taste her. First one breast, then the other, his mouth moved over her sensitized skin, licking, nibbling, suck-ling. The warm, tantalizing scent of her wrapped around him, driving him mad with a hunger he had only known with Lacy.

She clutched at his shoulders and lifted those long legs of hers to wrap around his waist. Having her there, in his arms, was so…*right.*

He cupped her bare bottom and held her steady as she looked into his eyes, showing him the passion, the desire that he knew was glittering in his own.

"Sam, Sam…" she asked, her voice breathless, "what're we doing?"

"What we were *meant* to do," he murmured, dip-ping his head to nibble at the slender length of her neck.

She shivered and that tiny reaction reverberated in-side him, setting off what felt like earthquake after-shocks that rippled through his system. Who would have guessed that as great as his memories of her had been, they weren't even *close* to how good she felt in reality.

Her fingers threaded through his hair and she pulled his head back to meet his gaze. "What're we waiting for, then?"

"No more waiting at all," he ground out.

Sam squeezed and caressed her behind until she was writhing against him and every twist of her hips hard-ened his body further until he felt as though he'd ex-plode with one wrong move. *Not yet,* his brain screamed, but his body was in charge now and rational or logical or *slow* didn't come into it.

Two long years it had been since he'd touched her last and now that he had her—naked, willing, wanting—he couldn't wait any longer.

Lacy, it seemed, felt the same. She shook her long hair back from her face, kissed him hard and deep, then reached down to undo his fly. Buttons sprang free under her fingers and in a second, she was holding him, stroking him from base to tip and back again. Sam gritted his teeth, struggling for control and losing, since he felt as wild as a hormonal teenager.

Need was a living, breathing animal in the room, snapping its jaws, demanding release. Sam's brain blanked out, every thought whipping away in the surge of his reaction to her touch. With her fingertips smoothing over him, he couldn't think beyond breathing. That was all he needed anyway. Air—and Lacy.

Shifting his grip on her, he stroked the hot, damp core of her. She sucked in a breath and trembled, but she didn't release her hold on him. If anything, her grip tightened, her caresses became more determined, more demanding. As did his. He rubbed the small bud of sensation at her center and each time she quivered and moaned, it fed his need to touch her more deeply. More completely.

She twisted in his grasp; her heels dug into the small of his back. "Sam, if you don't take me right this minute, I might die."

"No dying allowed," he muttered, and fused his mouth to hers. Their tongues tangled together again, even more desperately this time.

He'd come here with the idea to either talk through the barriers standing between them or seduce her into a sexual haze. Now neither one was happening. This wasn't seduction. It was raw urgency. Sam took two long steps to the closest wall, braced her back against it and then broke the kiss so he could look into her eyes as he filled her in one long, hard stroke.

She gasped and he was forced to pause, willing himself to be still. She was so tight. So hot, it stole his breath and left him gasping. A moment passed, and then as if of one mind they moved together, Lacy taking him deep inside her and each of them groaning when he retreated only to slide back inside, even deeper.

Again and again, they moved frantically, the rhythm they set a punishing pace that left no margin for smooth, for slow, lazy loving. It was all passion and lust and a desperate craving for the release that rose within them, higher and higher as they chased it. Emotion, sensation poured through them both, and then were drowned in the immediate demands of bodies too long denied.

He felt the cold of the wall on the palms of his hands as he braced her there, pinned like a butterfly to a board. He felt her fingers, digging into his shoulders as she urged him higher, faster, deeper. He heard their breaths coming fast and sharp.

Sam reached between their laboring bodies and flicked his thumb across that tight, sensitive bud at the junction of her thighs. Instantly, she screamed out his name as she shuddered, splintering in his arms.

Her body tightened around his; those internal shivers driving him over the edge. When the first explosion took him, Sam groaned aloud and emptied himself into her.

Seconds, minutes…maybe *days* passed with neither of them willing to move. Frankly, Sam didn't think he could move even if he had to. His knees were weak and the only thing holding them both up at the moment was sheer willpower.

"Oh. Wow." Her voice was a whisper that sounded like a shout to him. "Sam. I think I might be blind."

He looked at her. "Open your eyes."

She did. "Right. Good. Wow."

"You said that already," he told her, hissing in a

breath as she moved on him and sent his still-willing body into overdrive.

Nodding, Lacy murmured, "It was two *Wows* worthy."

"Yeah," he agreed, slapping one hand to her butt to try to hold her still. "Gotta say it really was."

Breathing still strained, Lacy looked at him and said, "I should probably tell you to leave now."

"Probably," he agreed, even as he felt his body hardening inside her again.

She felt it, too, because she inhaled sharply and let that breath slide from her on a soft moan of pleasure. "But I'm not."

"Glad to hear it." Sam tightened his grip on her, swung her away from the wall and walked, their bodies still linked, to the hall. "Bedroom?"

"Yeah," she said, dipping her head for another taste of his mouth. "Bedroom."

It was a small cabin and Sam took a moment to be grateful for that. He laid her down on the bed they used to share and reluctantly drew out of her heat just long enough to strip out of his clothes. Then he was back on the bed, looming over her, sheathing himself inside her on a sigh of appreciation. His hips moved as he reclaimed her body in the most elemental way. She met his pace and rocked with him in a dance they'd always been good at. Their rhythms meshed, their breaths mingled and the sighs crashing in the quiet seemed to roll on forever.

Lifting her legs, she locked them at the small of his back and pulled him tighter, deeper. She groaned as he kissed first one hardened nipple then the other, sending a cascade of sensations pouring into her body. Again and again, he licked, tasted, nibbled, all the while his body rocked into her heat, taking her as she took him.

There was no hesitation. No question. There was only the moment and the moment was *now*. They'd been heading toward this night since Sam had arrived back on the mountain.

Her hands swept up and down his back, her short, neat nails scraping at his skin as she touched him, everywhere. Her scent rose up and enveloped him. Surrounded by her, in her, Sam pushed them both to the brink of oblivion, and when she cried out his name, she held him tight and took him over the edge with her.

<u>Six</u>

Lacy stared up at the ceiling and, just for a second or two, enjoyed the lovely, floaty feeling that filled her. It had been so long since she'd felt anything like this. For the past two years, she'd forced herself to forget just how good it had always been between her and Sam. She'd had to, to survive his absence. Had to put it out of her mind so that she could try to rebuild her life without him.

Now he was back.

And in her bed.

God, how could she be such an idiot? Those lovely sensations of completion and satisfaction emptied away like water going down a tub drain.

"We should talk."

A short, sharp laugh shot from her throat. "Oh, I so don't want to talk about this." She wanted to forget again. Fast.

He went up on one elbow, looked down at her, and Lacy steeled herself against the gleam in his grass-green eyes. If she wasn't careful, her oh-so-foolish heart would slide gleefully right into danger. Why did he have to come back?

Why did he ever leave?

His jaw tight, he stared into her eyes and asked, "You're still taking the Pill, right?"

She blinked at him. Not what she'd been expecting. Yet, now that he'd said it, a single, slender thread of panic began to unwind inside her. His words echoed over and over again in her mind, because now her stupidity had reached epic proportions. Sam Wyatt walked in her door and every brain cell she possessed just whipped away. Which explained why she hadn't thought of protection. Hadn't paid any attention. She really was an idiot.

"Since you just went white," he said wryly, "I'm guessing the answer is no."

"Well, now's a great time to ask," she muttered, wishing she could blame this situation on him, as well. But she was a grown-up, modern woman who took responsibility for her own body, thanks very much. So it was as much her fault as his that she was suddenly thinking she might be in really big trouble here.

"We didn't do much talking before."

"True." She sighed and stared at the ceiling again. Easier than meeting his eyes. Easier than looking at him while she was wondering if she might have just gotten pregnant by her ex-husband. At that thought, she slapped one hand over her eyes.

Unprotected sex. She had never once—even at seventeen when she'd given Sam her virginity at the top of the mountain under a full, summer moon—been that reckless. Lacy was the careful one. The cautious one. The one who looked at every step along a path before she ever started down it. Now she couldn't even see the path. Oh, this was a mistake on so many levels she couldn't even count them all.

He pulled her hand aside and she looked at him.

"Now we have even more to talk about."

"No thanks." She didn't want to have a conversation with him at all. And certainly not about the possibility of an unplanned baby. *Oh, God.*

No way would fate do that to her, right? Hadn't it screwed with her life enough?

"No thanks?" He repeated her words with a snort of derision. "That's not gonna cover it. We just had sex. Twice. With zero protection."

"Yeah, I was there."

"Damn it, Lacy—"

"Look," she cut him off neatly and tried to get him off the subject, away from the thoughts that were already making her a little crazy. "It's the wrong time for me. The odds are astronomical." Please let her be right about this. "So don't worry about it, all right?"

He didn't like that. She could see the light in his eyes and recognized it. Sam Wyatt never had been a man to be told what to do and take it well.

"Yeah," he said flatly. "That's not gonna happen. I want to know when you know."

"And I want a brand-new camera with a fifteen-zoom lens. Looks like we're both going to be disappointed."

"Damn it, Lacy," he repeated. "You can't cut me out of this. I'm here. I'm involved in this."

"For now." A part of her couldn't believe that she was lying in bed with Sam, both of them naked and having an argument about a possible pregnancy. That was the sane part, she thought reasonably. The panicked portion of her was trying not to think about any of this.

Once he left the cabin she wouldn't be bringing up tonight with him at all. And she was going to use every part of her legendary focus to forget everything that had just happened—mainly out of self-protection. She couldn't think about being with him and *not* be with him. That was a recipe for even more craziness and more late-night crying sessions, so thanks, she'd pass.

When she didn't speak, he seemed to accept her silence as acquiescence, which worked for her—until he started talking again.

"I came over here tonight to talk to you," he said.

"Yeah," she said on a sigh, "that went well."

"Okay," he admitted, "maybe talking wasn't the only thing on my mind." He dropped one hand to her hip and slowly slid his palm up until he was cupping her breast, sending tingles of expectation and licks of heat sinking down into her bones.

Just not fair, she told herself sternly even as she felt that heat he engendered begin to spread. Not fair that the man who broke her heart could still have such an effect on her. Even when she *knew* it was a mistake to allow his hands on her, she couldn't bring herself to make him stop. And if she kept lying there, letting him touch her, it would start over again and where would that get her? Deeper into the hole she could already feel herself falling into.

Quickly, before she could talk herself out of doing the smart thing, she rolled out from under his hand and off the bed in one fluid motion. Just getting a little distance between them cleared her mind and soothed all those buzzing nerve endings.

He stared at her as she snatched up the robe she had

tossed over a chair only that morning. Slipping into the soft terry fabric she tied it at the waist and only briefly considered making a knot, just to make it harder to slip off again. Once she was covered up, Lacy felt a bit more in control. Tossing her hair back from her face, she said, "I think you should go."

"I came to talk, remember? We haven't done that yet."

"And we're not going to," she told him. "I don't feel like talking and you don't live here anymore, so I want you to go."

"As soon as we have this out." He settled on the bed, carelessly naked, clearly in no hurry to get up and get moving. "I've got a few things to say to you."

"Now you have things to say? *Now* you want to share?" She laughed shortly and the sound of it was as harsh as the scrape of it against her throat. Through the miasma of emotions coursing through her, rage rose up and buried everything else. "Two years ago, you left without a word of explanation. Just came home from the funeral, threw some clothes in your bag and went."

In a blink, she was back there. In this very cabin two years ago when her world had come crashing down around her.

The funeral had been hideous. Losing Jack to a senseless accident after he'd survived cancer had cut deeper than she would have thought possible. The Wyatt family had closed ranks, of course, pulling into a tight circle where pain shared had become pain more easily borne.

All of them but Sam. Even within that circle, he had stood apart, forcing himself to be stoic. To be solitary. He hadn't turned to Lacy once for comfort, for solace.

Instead, he'd handled all of the funeral arrangements himself, taken care of details to keep his parents from having to multiply their grief by dealing with the minutia of death. He'd given the eulogy and brought everyone to tears and laughter with memories of his twin.

But after everyone had gone home, after the ceremony had faded into stillness, she'd hoped he would finally turn to her.

He hadn't.

Instead he walked straight into their bedroom and pulled his travel bag out of the closet.

Stunned, shaken, Lacy could only watch as he grabbed shirts, rolled them up and stuffed them into the bag. Jeans were next, then underwear, socks and still she didn't speak. But as he zipped it closed and stood staring down at the bag, she asked, "Sam, what are you doing? Are we going somewhere?"

He looked at her then and his green eyes were drenched with a sorrow so deep it tore at her to see it. "Not *we*, Lacy. *Me*. I'm going. I have to—"

She swallowed hard against the knot in her throat. "You're leaving?"

"Yeah." He stripped out of his black suit, and quickly dressed in boots, jeans and a thermal shirt, then shrugged into his leather jacket

The whole time, she could only watch him. Her mind had gone entirely blank. It couldn't be happening. He had promised her long ago that he would never leave. That she would always be able to count on him. To trust him. So none of this made sense. She couldn't understand. Didn't believe he would do this.

"You're leaving me?"

He snapped her a look that said everything and nothing. "I have to go."

She couldn't breathe. Iron bands tightened around her chest, cutting off her air. It had to be a dream. A nightmare, because Sam wouldn't leave. He walked across the room then, his duffel swung over one shoulder, and she stepped back, allowing him to pass because she was too stunned to try to stop him.

He stopped at the front door for one last look at her. "Take care of yourself, Lacy." He left without another word and closed the door behind him quietly.

Alone in her cabin, Lacy sank to the floor, since her knees were suddenly water. She watched the door for a long time, waiting for it to open again, for him to come back, tell her he'd made a mistake. But he never did.

Now, thinking about that night, Lacy wanted to kick her former self for letting him stroll out of her life. For crying for him. For missing him. For hoping to God he'd just come home.

"I had to."

"Yeah," she said tightly, amazed that as angry as she was, there was still more anger bubbling inside her. "You said that then, too. You *had* to leave your wife, your family." Sarcasm came thick. "Wow, must have been rough on you. All on your own, free of your pesky wife and those irritating parents and sister. Wandering across Europe, dating royalty. Poor little you, how you must have suffered."

"Wasn't why I left," he ground out, and Lacy was pleased to see a matching anger begin to glint in his eyes. A good old-fashioned argument was at least honest.

"Just a great side benefit, then?"

"Lacy I couldn't explain then why I had to leave—"

"Couldn't?" she asked. "Or wouldn't?"

"I could hardly breathe, Lacy," he muttered, sitting up to shove both hands through his hair in irritation. "I needed space. It had nothing to do with you or the family."

Lacy jerked back as if he'd slapped her. "Really? That's how you see it? It had everything to do with us. You couldn't breathe because your family needed you? Poor baby. That's called *life*, Sam. Bad stuff happens. It's how we deal with it that decides who we are."

"And I didn't deal."

"No," she said flatly. "You didn't. You ran. *We* were the ones left behind to sweep up the pieces of our lives. Not you, Sam. You were gone."

His mouth worked as if he were trying to hold back words just itching to pour out. "I didn't run."

"That's what it looked like from the cheap seats."

Nodding, he could have been agreeing or trying to rein in his own temper. "You didn't say any of this at the time."

"How could I? You wouldn't *talk* to me," she countered. "You were in such a rush to get out of the cabin, you hardly saw me, Sam. So you can understand that the fact you want me to be all cooperative because *now* you want to talk, is just a little too much for me."

Scowling at her, he wondered aloud, "What happened to quiet, shy Lacy who never lost her temper?"

She flushed and hoped the room was dark enough to disguise it. "Her husband walked out on her and she grew a spine."

"However it happened, I like it."

"Hah!" Startled by the out-of-the-blue compliment when she was in no way interested in flattery from him, Lacy muttered, "I don't care."

He blew out a breath and said, "You think I wanted to go."

"I know you did." She could still feel his sense of eagerness to be gone. Out of the cabin. Away from her.

"Damn it, Lacy, Jack *died*."

"And we all lost him, Sam," she pointed out hotly. "You weren't the only one in pain."

He jumped off the bed and stood across from it, facing her. "He was my twin. My identical twin. Losing him was like losing a part of me."

Torn between empathy for the pain he so clearly still felt and fury that he would think she didn't understand, she blurted out, "Did you think I didn't know that? That your parents, your sister, were clueless as to what Jack's death cost you?" Her voice climbed on every word until she heard herself shouting and deliberately dialed it back. "We were here for you, Sam. You didn't see us."

"I couldn't." He shook his head, glanced around for his clothes, then reached down and snatched up his jeans. Tugging them on, he left them unbuttoned as he faced her again. "Hell, I was half out of my mind with grief and rage. I couldn't be around you."

"Ah," she said, nodding sagely as she silently congratulated herself for not throwing something at him. "So you left for *my* sake. How heroic."

"Damn it, you're not listening to me."

"No, I'm not. Not much fun being ignored, is it?" She gathered up her hair with trembling fingers and in a series of familiar moves, tamed the mass into a thick braid that frayed at the edges. "Why should I listen to you anyway?"

"Because I'm back now."

"For how long?"

He frowned again and shook his head. "I don't know the answer to that yet."

"So, just passing through." Wow, it was amazing how much that one statement hurt. And Lacy knew that if she allowed herself to get even more involved with him, when he left this time, the pain would be more than she could take. So she drew a cloak of disinterest around her and belted it as tightly as her robe. "Well, have a nice trip to…wherever."

The pain was as thick and rich as it had been two years ago. She'd gotten through it then, curling up in solitude, focusing on her job at the lodge and on her photography. The pictures she'd taken during that time were black-and-white and filled with shadows that seemed to envelop the landscape. She could look at them now and actually *feel* the misery she'd been living through. And damned if she would go back to that dark place in her life.

He took a breath and huffed it out again in a burst of frustration. "I'm not proud of what I did two years ago, Lacy. But I had to go, whether you believe that or not."

"I'm sure you believe it," she countered.

"And I'm—"

"Don't you dare say you're sorry." Her voice cracked into the room like a whip's snap.

"I won't. I did what I had to do at the time." His features were tight, his eyes shining with an emotion she couldn't read in the dim light. "Can't be sorry for it now."

Flabbergasted, Lacy stared at him and actually felt her jaw drop. "That's amazing. Really. You're *not* sorry, are you?"

Again, he pushed his hands through his hair and

looked suddenly as if he'd rather be anywhere but there. "What good would it do?"

"Not an answer," she pointed out.

"All I can give you."

Cold. She was cold. And her thick terry-cloth robe might as well have been satin for all the warmth it was providing at the moment. For two years, she'd thought about what it might be like if he ever came home. If he ever deigned to return to the family he'd torn apart with his absence. But somehow, she'd always imagined that he'd come back contrite. Full of regret.

She should have known better. Sam Wyatt did what he wanted when he wanted and explained himself to no one. Heck, she'd known him most of her life, had married him, and he'd still kept a part of himself locked away where she couldn't touch it. He'd gone his own way always and for a while, he'd taken her with him. And she, Lacy thought with a flash of disgust, had been so glad to be included, she'd never pushed for more— that was her fault. His leaving? His fault.

"God," he said on a short laugh, "I can practically *see* you thinking. Why don't you just say what you have to and get it out?"

"Wow. You really have not changed one bit, have you?"

"What's that supposed to mean?"

"You even want to be in charge of when I unload on you."

"We both know you've got something to say, so say it and get it done."

"You want it?" she asked, hands fisting helplessly at her sides. "Fine. You walked out on all of us, Sam. You walked away from a family who loved you. Needed you. You walked away from *me*. You never said goodbye.

You just disappeared and then the next thing I know, divorce papers are arriving in the mail."

He blew out a breath.

"You didn't even warn me with a stinking phone call." Outrage fired in her chest and sizzled in her veins. "You vanished and Jack was dead and your family was shattered and you didn't care."

"Of course I cared," he snapped.

"If you cared, you wouldn't have left. Now you're back and you're what? A hero? The prodigal returned at last? Sorry you didn't get a parade."

"I didn't expect—"

She rolled right over him. "Two years. A few postcards to let your parents know you were alive and that was it. What the hell were you thinking? How could you be so heartless to people who needed you?"

He scrubbed both hands over his face as if he could wipe away the impact of her words, but Lacy wasn't finished.

Her voice dropping to a heated whisper that was nearly lost beneath the moan of the icy wind outside, she said, "You broke my heart, Sam. You broke *me*." She slapped one hand to her chest and glared at him from across the room. "I trusted you. I believed you when you said it was forever. And then you left me."

Just like her mother had left, Lacy thought, her brain firing off scattershot images, memories that stole her breath and weakened her knees. When she was ten years old, Lacy's mother had walked away from the mountain, from her husband and daughter, and she had never once looked back. Never once gotten in touch. Not a phone call. Or a letter. Nothing. As if she'd slipped off the edge of the earth.

Lacy had spent the rest of her childhood hoping and

waiting for her mom to come home. But she never had, and though he'd stayed, Lacy's father had slowly, inexorably pulled away, too. Lacy could see now that he hadn't meant to. But his wife leaving had diminished him to the point where he couldn't remain the man he had once been. Her family had been shattered.

And when Sam convinced her to trust him, to build a life with him and then left, she'd been shattered again. She wouldn't allow that to happen a third time. Lacy was stronger now. She'd had to change to survive and there was no going back.

"You know what? That's it. I'm done. We have to work together, Sam," she said. "For however long you're here. But that's all. Work."

"Damn it, Lacy…" His features were shadowed, but somehow the green of his eyes seemed to shine in the darkness. After a second or two, he nodded. "Fine. We'll leave it there. For now."

She was grateful they had that much settled, at least. Because if he tried to apologize for ripping her heart out of her chest, she might have to hit him with something. Something heavy. Better that they just skate over it all. She'd had her say and it was time to leave her scars alone.

"And what about what just happened?" he asked, and she wondered why his voice had to sound like dark chocolate. "What if you're pregnant?"

That word sent a shiver that might have been panic—or longing—skating along her spine. "I won't be."

"If you are," he warned, "we're not done."

Another flush swept through her, heating up the embers that had just been stoked into an inferno. "We're already done, Sam. Whatever we had, died two years ago."

Her whisper resounded in the room and she could only hope he didn't read the lie behind the words.

Because she knew, that no matter what happened, what was between them would never really die.

Two days later, Sam was still thinking about that night with Lacy.

Now, standing in the cold wind, staring up at the clear blue sky dotted with massive white clouds, his brain was free to wander. And as always, it went straight to Lacy.

Everything she'd said to him kept replaying through his mind and her image was seared into his memory. He'd never forget how she'd looked, standing there in her robe, eyes glinting with fury, her mouth still full from his kisses. The old Lacy wouldn't have told him off—she'd have hugged her anger close and just looked...hurt.

What did it say about him that this new Lacy—full of fire and fury—intrigued him even more than the one he used to know?

Being with her again had hit him far harder than he had expected. The feel of her skin, the sound of her sighs, the brush of her lips on his. It was more than sexual, it was...*deeper* than that. She'd reclaimed that piece of his heart that he had excised so carefully two years before. And now he wasn't sure what to do about that.

Of course, he'd steered clear of the office for the past two days, giving himself the time and space to do some serious thinking. But so far, all he'd come up with was...he still wanted her.

Two years he'd denied himself what he most wanted—Lacy. Now she was within reach again and he wasn't about to deny himself any longer. She might think that what was between them had died…but if he had killed it, then he could resurrect it. He had to believe that, because the alternative was unacceptable.

He tossed a glance at the office window and considered going in to—what? Talk? No, he wasn't interested in more conversation that simply ended up being a circular argument. And what he *was* interested in couldn't be done in the office when anyone could walk in on them. So he determinedly pushed aside those thoughts and focused instead on work. On his plans.

Sam walked into the lodge and headed straight through the lobby for the elevator. He paid no attention to the people gathered in front of a blazing fire or the hum of conversations rising and falling. There were a few things he needed to go over with his father. One idea in particular had caught his imagination and he wanted to run it past his dad.

He found the older man in his favorite chair in the family great room. But for the murmuring of the TV, the house was quiet and Sam was grateful for the reprieve. He wasn't in the mood to face Kristi's antagonism or his mother's quiet reproach.

"Hey, Sam," his father said, giving a quick look around as if checking to make sure his wife wasn't around. "How about a beer?"

Sam grinned. His father had the look of a desperate man. "Mom okay with that?"

"No, she's not," he admitted with a grimace. "But since you got home, she's stocked the fridge. So while she's in town, we could take advantage."

He looked so damn hopeful, Sam didn't have the heart to shoot him down. "Sure, Dad. I'll risk it with you."

His father slapped his hands together, then gave them

a quick rub in anticipation. Pushing out of his chair, he led the way to the kitchen, his steps long and sure. It was good to see his father more himself. Bob Wyatt wasn't the kind of man to take to sitting in a recliner for long. The inactivity alone would kill him.

In the kitchen, Sam took a seat at the round oak table and waited while his dad pulled two bottles of beer out of the fridge. He handed one to Sam, kept the other for himself and sat down. Twisting off the top, Bob took a long drink, sighed in pleasure and gave his son a wide smile. "Your mother's so determined to have me eating tree bark and drinking healthy sludge, this beer's like a vacation."

"Yeah," Sam said, taking a sip of his own, "but if she comes in suddenly, you're on your own."

"Coward."

Sam grinned. "Absolutely."

With a good-natured shrug, Bob said, "Can't blame you. So, want to tell me why you're stopping by in the middle of the day?"

He couldn't very well admit to avoiding Lacy, so Sam went right to the point. "You know we've got a lot of plans in motion for the resort."

"Yeah." Bob took another sip and nodded. "I've got to say you've got some good ideas, Sam. I like your plan so far, though I'm a little concerned about just how much of your own money you're pumping into this place."

"Don't worry about that." Sam had enough money to last several lifetimes, and if he couldn't enjoy spending it, what was the point of accruing it?

"Well," his father said, "I'll keep worrying over it and you'll keep spending, so we all do what we can."

Sam grinned again. God, he hadn't even realized

how much he'd missed being able to sit down and talk to his dad. Just the simplicity of being in this kitchen again, sharing a beer with the man who had raised him, eased a lot of the still-jagged edges inside him.

"If you like the plans so far, you'll like this one, too." Sam cupped the beer bottle between his palms and took a second to get his thoughts in order. While he did, he glanced around the familiar kitchen.

Pale green walls, white cabinets and black granite countertops, this room had been the heart of the Wyatt family for years. Hell, he, Jack and Kristi had all sat around this table doing homework before the requisite family dinner. This room had witnessed arguments, laughter and tears. It was the gathering place where everyone came when they needed to be heard. To be loved.

"Sam?"

"Yeah. Sorry." He shook his head and gave a rueful smile. "Lots of memories here."

"Thick as honey," his father agreed. "More good than bad, though."

"True." Even when Jack was going through cancer treatment, the family would end up here, giving each other the strength to keep going. He could almost hear his brother's laughter and the pain of that memory etched itself onto his soul.

"You're not the only one who misses him, you know." His father's voice was soft, low.

"Sometimes," Sam admitted on a sigh, "I still expect him to walk into the room laughing, telling me it was all a big mistake."

"Being here makes it easier and harder all at the same time," his father said softly. "Because even if I can fool myself at times, when I see his chair at the table sitting empty, I have to acknowledge that's he's really gone."

Sam's gaze shot to that chair now.

"But the good memories are stronger than the pain and that's a comfort when you let it be."

"You think I don't want to be comforted?" Sam looked at his father.

"I think when Jack died you decided you weren't allowed to be happy."

Stunned, Sam didn't say anything.

"You take too much on yourself, Sam," Bob said. "You always did."

As he sipped his beer, Sam considered that and admitted silently that his father was right. About all of it. Maybe what had driven him from home wasn't only losing Jack and needing to see his twin's dreams realized—but the fact that he had believed, deep down, that with Jack gone, Sam didn't deserve to be happy. It was something to consider. Later.

Shaking his head, he said, "About this latest idea…"

Apparently accepting that Sam needed a change of subject, his father nodded. "What're you thinking?"

"I want to initiate a new beginner's ski run on the backside of the mountain," Sam said, jumping right in. "The slope's gentle, there're fewer trees and it's wide enough we could set it up to have two runs operating all the time."

"Yeah, there's a problem with that," Bob said, and took another drink of his beer.

The hesitation in his father's voice had Sam's internal radar lighting up. "What?"

"The thing is, that property doesn't belong to us anymore."

The radar was now blinking and shrieking inside him. "What're you talking about?"

"You know Lacy's family has lived on that slope for years…"

"Yeah…" Sam had the distinct feeling he wasn't going to like where this was going.

"Well, after you left, Lacy was in a bad way." Bob frowned as he said it and Sam knew his father was the master of understatement. Guilt pinged around inside him like a wildly ricocheting bullet. "So, your mother and I, we deeded the property to her. Felt like it was the least we could do to try to ease her hurt."

Sam muffled the groan building in his chest. His decision to leave was now coming back to bite him in so many different ways. Most especially with the woman he still wanted more than his next breath.

"So, if you're determined to build that beginner run, you're going to have to deal with Lacy."

Letting his head hit his chest, Sam realized that *dealing with Lacy* pretty much summed up his entire life at the moment. He thought about the look in her eyes when he left her cabin the other night. The misery stamped there despite what they'd just shared—hell, maybe *because* of that.

Leaving here was something he'd *had* to do. Coming back meant facing the consequences of that decision. It wasn't getting any easier.

"She never mentioned that you and mom gave her the land," Sam said.

"Any reason why she should?"

"No." Shaking his head, Sam took another pull on his beer. He wanted that land. How he was going to get it from Lacy, he didn't know yet. As things stood between them at the moment, he was sure that she would never sell him that slope. And maybe it'd be best to just forget about getting his hands on it. The land was Lacy's, and he ought to back off. But for now, there were other things he wanted to talk to his father about. "You know that photo of the lodge in spring? The one hanging over the fireplace here?"

"Yeah, what about it?"

"I'd like to use it on the new website I'm having designed so I'll need to talk to the photographer. I want to show the lodge in all the seasons with photos that rotate out, always changing. The one I'm talking about now, with Mom's tulips a riot of color and that splash of deep blue sky—the picture really shows the lodge in a great way."

"It's one of Lacy's."

Sam looked at his dad for a long moment, then actually laughed, unsurprised. "Of course it is. Just like I suppose the shot of the lodge in winter, with the Christmas tree in the front window is hers, too?"

His father nodded, a smile tugging at the corner of his mouth as he took a sip of his beer. "You got it. She's made a name for herself in the last year or so. We've had hotel guests buy the photos right off the walls." He shook his head, smiling to himself. "Lacy does us up some extra prints just so we can accommodate the tourists. She's been making some good money selling her photos through a gallery in Ogden, too."

"She never mentioned it."

And it was weird to realize that he was so out of touch with Lacy. There had been a time when they were so close, nothing between them was secret. Now there was an entire chunk of her life that he knew nothing about. His own damn fault and he knew it, but that didn't make it any easier to choke down.

His father nodded sagely. "Uh-huh. Again, any reason why she should have?"

"No." Blowing out a breath in frustration, Sam leaned back in his kitchen chair and studied his father. There was a sly expression on the older man's face that told Sam his father was enjoying this. "She doesn't owe me a thing. I get that. But damn it, we shared a lot of great times, too. Don't they mean something? Okay fine. I left. But I'm back now. That counts, too, doesn't it?"

"It does with me. Lacy may be harder to convince."

"I know."

"And Kristi."

"I know." Sam snorted. "And Mom."

Bob winced. "Your mother's damn happy to have you back, Sam."

"Yeah," he said, turning his head to look out the window at the pockets of deep blue sky visible between the pines. He'd felt it from his mom since he'd returned. The reluctance to be too excited to see him. The wary pleasure at having him home. "But she's also holding back, waiting for me to go again."

"And are you?"

Guilt reared up and gnawed at the edges of his heart. "I don't know yet. Wish I did. But I promised you I'd stay at least until these plans are complete and the way I'm adding things I might never be finished."

"All true," his father said. "You might ask yourself sometime why it is you keep thinking of more things to do. More things that will give you an excuse to stay here longer."

He hadn't thought of it like that but now that he was, Sam could see that maybe subconsciously he had been working toward coming home for good. Funny that he hadn't noticed that the more involved his plans became the further out he pushed the idea of leaving again.

"Anyway," his father said, "while you're doing all this thinking, you'll have to talk to Lacy about using her photos in the advertising you're planning."

"I will," he said.

"She's really good, isn't she?"

"She always was," Sam acknowledged and knew he was talking about much more than her talent for photography.

Seven

"You want to use my photos?"

Sam grinned at Lacy an hour later and told himself it was good to actually surprise her. He enjoyed how her eyes went wide and her mouth dropped open.

"I do. And not just on the website, I'd like to use them in print advertising, as well."

"Why—"

He tipped his head. "Don't pretend you don't know how good a photographer you are."

"I don't know how to respond to that without sounding conceited."

"Well, while you're quiet, here's something else to think about." He planted both palms on the edge of the desk and leaned in until he was eye to eye with her. "I'll want some of your photos made into postcards that we can sell in the lobby of the lodge."

"Postcards."

"Hey, some people actually enjoy *real* mail," he told

her and straightened up. "We can have a lawyer draw up terms—all nice and legal, but I'm thinking a seventy-thirty split, your favor, on the cards and any prints we sell. As for the advertising, we'll call that a royalty deal and you'll get a cut every time we use one of your photos."

She blinked at him and damned if he didn't enjoy having her off balance. "Royalty."

Sam leaned over, tipped her chin up with his fingers and bent to plant a hard, quick kiss on her mouth. While she was flustered from that, he straightened up and announced, "Why don't you think it over? I'm heading out to meet with the architect. Be back later."

He left her staring after him. His own heart was thundering in his chest and every square inch of his body was coiled tight as an overwound spring. Just being around her made him want everything he'd once walked away from.

Sam shrugged into his jacket as he left the hotel and headed out into a yard that boasted green splotches of grass where the snow was melting under a steady sun. He took a deep breath, glanced around at the people and realized that it had taken him two years of being away to discover that his place was *here*.

His life was here.

And he wanted Lacy in his life again. Smiling to himself, Sam decided he was going to romance the hell out of her until he got just what he wanted. That slope he needed for the lodge expansion was going to have to wait, he told himself as he headed for his car. Because if Lacy found out he wanted the property she owned, she would never believe he wanted her for herself.

Lacy's nose wrinkled at the rich, dark scent of the latte Kristi carried as the two of them walked along

Historic Twenty-Fifth Street in downtown Ogden. The street was narrow with cars parked in front of brick and stone buildings that had been standing for more than a hundred years. Twenty-Fifth Street had begun life as the welcome mat for train travelers, then it morphed into a wild blend of bars and brothels.

But in the 1950s, it had been reborn as a destination for shopping and dining, and today, it retained all of the old-world charm while it boasted eclectic shops and restaurants that drew tourists from all over. And depending on the time of year, Historic Twenty-Fifth hosted farmer's markets, art festivals, Pioneer Days, Witchstock and even a Christmas village.

Lacy loved it, and usually, strolling along the street and peeking into storefronts cheered her up. But today, she was forcing herself into this trip with Kristi.

"Since when do you say no to coffee?" her friend asked after another sip of her latte.

"Since my stomach's not so sure it approves of food anymore." She swallowed hard, took a deep breath and hoped the fresh air would settle her stomach.

"Well, that sucks," her friend said, shrugging deeper into her jacket as a cold wind shot down the street as if determined to remind everyone that winter wasn't over yet. "Something you ate?"

"Hopefully," Lacy murmured. She didn't want to think about other causes of her less than happy stomach. It had been two weeks since her night with Sam and she couldn't help but think that her sudden bouts of queasiness had more to do with a nine-month flu than anything else. Still, she didn't want to share any of this with Kristi yet, so more loudly, she said, "It's probably the cold pizza I had for dinner last night."

"That'd do it for me," Kristi acknowledged with a

grimace. "You do know how to use a microwave, right? Now that we've struggled out of the caves there is no need to settle for cold pepperoni."

"I'll make a note." They passed a gift store, its front window crowded with pretty pots of flowers, gardening gloves and a barbecue apron that proudly demanded Kiss The Cook, all lovely promises of spring. But the sky was overcast and the wind whistling down from Powder Mountain, looming over the end of the street, made the thought of spring seem like a fairy tale.

Unwell or not, it was good to be away from Snow Vista, wandering down Ogden's main street where she had absolutely zero chance of running into Sam. The man hadn't left the mountain since he got back. And for the past two weeks, she'd hardly spoken to him at all. After that wild bout of earth-shattering sex, Lacy had figured he'd be back wanting more—heaven knew she did. But he'd kept his distance and she knew she should be grateful. Instead, she was irritated.

"So you want to tell me what's going on between you and Sam these days?"

Kristi's question jolted Lacy and her steps faltered for a second. This woman had been her best friend for years. There was nothing they hadn't shared with each other, from first kisses to loss of virginity and beyond. Yet, Lacy just didn't feel comfortable talking about Sam right now. Especially with his little sister.

She gave a deliberate shrug. "Nothing. Why?"

"Please," Kristi said with a snort. "I'm not speaking to him, either, but *you're* not speaking to him really loudly."

"That doesn't even make sense." Lacy paused outside the cupcake shop to stare wistfully at a rainbow confetti cupcake. Normally, she would have gone in and bought herself one. Or a dozen. Today, though, it didn't seem like a good idea to feed her already-iffy stomach that much sugar. Just the pizza she'd eaten, she told herself. She'd be fine in a day or two.

"Sure it does. Mom says you were at the house a couple days ago, visiting Dad. And when Sam showed up you left so fast there were sparks coming up from your boot heels."

Lacy sighed. "Your mom's great but she exaggerates."

"I've seen those sparks, too, when you're in full retreat." Kristi gave her a friendly arm bump as they walked. "I know it's probably hardest on you, Sam being back and everything. But I thought you were over him. You *said* you were over him."

"I exaggerate, too," Lacy mumbled and stopped at the corner, waiting for a green light to cross the street. Her gaze swept along the street.

One of the things she liked best about Ogden was that it protected its history. Relished it. The buildings were updated to be safe, but the heart and soul of them remained to give the downtown area a sense of the past even as it embraced the future.

At the end of the street stood the Ogden train station. Restored to its beautiful Spanish Colonial Revival style, it boasted a gorgeous clock tower in the center of the building. Inside, she knew, were polished wood, high-beamed ceilings and wall murals done by the same artist who did the Ellis Island murals in the 1930s.

Today there was an arts-and-crafts fair going on inside, and she and Kristi were headed there to check out the booths and see how Lacy's photographs were selling.

"I knew you weren't over him," Kristi said with just a touch of a smug smile. "I told you. You still love him."

"No. I won't." Lacy stopped, took a breath. "I mean I don't." She wanted to mean it, even as she felt herself weakening. What kind of an idiot, after all, would she be to deliberately set herself up to get run over again? The light turned green and both women crossed the street.

"Any decent self-help book would tell you that what you just said has flags flying all over it." Still smug, Kristi gave Lacy a smile and took another drink of her latte. "You're trying so hard, but it's hopeless. You do love him—you just don't want to love him. Or forgive him. And I so get that." Shaking her head, Kristi added, "Tony keeps telling me that I've got to let it go. Accept that Sam did what he had to do just like we did. We all stayed and he had to go. Simple."

"Doesn't it just figure that a guy would defend another guy?"

"That's what I thought, too," Kristi admitted. "But in a way, he has a point."

Lacy snorted. "Hard to believe that Sam *had* to leave."

"Yeah," Kristi said on a sigh, and crossed the street, matching her strides to Lacy's. "That urge to bolt out of a hard situation was really more Jack than Sam. Jack never could stand any really deep emotional thing. If a woman cried around him, he'd vanish in a blink."

"I remember," Lacy said wistfully. Hadn't they all teased Jack about his inability to handle any relationship that looked deeper than a puddle?

"I love both of my brothers," Kristi told her, "but I always knew that Sam was the dependable one. Jack was fun—God, he was fun!" Her smile was wide for a split second, then faded. "But you never knew if he'd be home for dinner or if he'd be on his way to Austria for the skiing instead."

Kristi was right. Sam had always been the responsible one. The one you could count on, Lacy thought. Which had made his leaving all that much harder to understand. To accept. As for forgiving, how did you forgive someone you had trusted above everyone else for breaking their word and your heart along with it?

"I kind of hate to admit it, but Tony may be right," Kristi was saying. "I mean, I'm still mad at Sam, but when I see him with Dad, it makes it harder to stay mad, you know?"

"Yeah, I do." That was part of her problem, Lacy thought. She so wanted to keep her sense of righteous anger burning bright, but every time she saw Sam with his father, she softened a little. When she watched him out on the slopes just yesterday, helping a little boy figure out how to make a parallel turn. When she saw him standing in the wind, talking future plans with the contractor. All of these images were fresh and new and starting to whittle away at the fury she had once been sure would be with her forever.

"Dad's so pleased he's back. He's recovering from that heart attack scare faster I think, because Sam's over every day and the two of them are continuously going over all of the plans for Snow Vista." She took another gulp of coffee and Lacy envied it. "Mom's a little cooler, almost as if, like you, she's half expecting him to disappear again, but even she's happy about Sam being home. I can see it in her eyes and on the bathroom scale since she's still cooking the fatted calf for her prodigal nearly every night. Maybe," Kristi said thoughtfully, "it would be easier to forgive and be glad he was here if I knew he was staying."

Lacy's ears perked up. Here was something important. Had he decided to stay after all? And if he did, what would that mean for her? For *them*?

"He hasn't said anything to any of you?"

"No. Just sort of does his work, visits with the parents and avoids all mention of the future—outside of the plans he's got cooking for the resort." Kristi tossed her now-empty cup into a trash can. "So every day I wait to hear that he's gone. He left so fast the last time—" She broke off and winced. "Sorry."

"Nothing to be sorry about," Lacy said as they walked up to the entrance of the train station. "He did leave, and yeah, I'm not convinced he's staying, either."

And she didn't know if that made her life easier or harder. If he was going to leave again, she had to keep her distance for her own heart's sake. She couldn't let herself care again. And if he was staying…what? Could she love him? Could she ever really trust him not to leave her behind again?

What if she didn't have the flu? What if she had gotten pregnant that one night with him? What then? Did she tell him or keep it to herself?

Feeling as if her head might explode, Lacy pushed it all to one side and walked into the train station, deliberately closing her mind to thoughts of Sam for the rest of the day. Instantly, she was slapped with the noise of hundreds of people, talking, laughing, shouting. There were young moms with babies in strollers and toddlers firmly in hand. There were a few men looking as if they'd rather be anywhere else, and then there were the grandmas, traveling in packs as they wandered the crowded station.

Lacy and Kristi paid their entrance fee and joined the herd of people streaming down the narrow aisles. There were so many booths it was hard to see everything at once, which meant that she and Kristi would be making several trips around the cavernous room.

"Oh, I love this." Kristi had already stopped to pick up a hand-worked wooden salad bowl, sanded and polished to a warm honeyed gleam. While she dickered with the artisan, Lacy wandered on. She studied dry floral wreaths, hand-painted front-door hangers shouting WELCOME SPRING and then deliberately hurried past a booth packed with baby bibs, tiny T-shirts and beautifully handmade cradles.

She wouldn't think about it. Not until she had to. And if there was a small part of her that loved the chance that she might be pregnant, she wasn't going to indulge that tiny, wistful voice in the back of her mind.

Lacy dawdled over the jewelry exhibit and then the hand-tooled leather journals. She stopped at the Sweet and Salty booth and looked over the bags of snacks. Her stomach was still unhappy, so she bought a small bag of plain popcorn, hoping it would help. Nibbling as she went, her gaze swept over the area. There were paintings, blown-glass vases and wineglasses, kids' toys and outdoor furniture made by real craftsmen. But she moved through the crowd with her destination in mind. The local art gallery had a booth at the fair every year and that's where Lacy was headed. She sold her photographs through the gallery and she liked to keep track of what kind of photos sold best.

She loved her job at the lodge, enjoyed teaching kids how to ski, but taking photographs, capturing moments, was her real love. Lacy nibbled at the popcorn as she climbed the steps to the gallery's display. The owner was busy dealing with a customer, so Lacy busied herself, studying the shots that were displayed alongside beautiful oil paintings, watercolors and pastels.

Seeing her shots of the mountain, of sunrises and sunsets, of an iced-over lake, gave her the same thrill it always did. Here was her heart. Taking photographs, finding just the right way to tell a story in a picture— that was what fed her soul. And now, she reminded herself, Sam wanted to use her work to advertise the resort. She was flattered and touched and sliding down that slippery slope toward caring for him again.

The owner of the gallery, Heather Burke, handed Lacy's black-and-white study of a snow-laden pine tree to a well-dressed woman carrying a gorgeous blueberry-colored leather bag.

Pride rippled through Lacy. People valued her work. Not just Sam and those at the lodge, but strangers, people who looked at her prints and saw art or beauty or memories. And that was a gift, she thought. Knowing that others appreciated the glimpses of nature that she froze in time.

Lacy smiled at Heather as the woman approached, a look of satisfaction on her face. "I loved that picture."

"So did she," Heather said with a wink. "Enough to pay three hundred for it."

"Three hundred?" The amount was surprising, though Heather had always insisted that Lacy priced her shots too low. "Seriously?"

"Yes, seriously." Heather laughed delightedly. "And, I sold your shot of the little boy skating on the ice rink for two."

"Wow." Exciting, and even better, if she did turn out to be pregnant, at least she knew she wouldn't have to worry about making enough money to take care of her child.

"I told you people are willing to pay for beautiful things, Lacy. And," Heather added meaningfully, "now that spring and summer tourists are almost here, I'm going to need more of your photographs for the gallery. My stock's getting low and we don't want to miss any sales, right?"

"Right. I'll get you more by next week."

"Great." Heather gave her an absent pat on the arm and whispered, "I've got another live one I think. Talk to you later." Then she swept in on an older man studying the photo of a lone skier, whipping down Snow Vista's peak.

Lacy's heart gave a little lurch as it always did when she saw that shot. It was Sam, of course, taken a few years ago just before the season opened and the two of them had had the slopes to themselves. In the photo, the snow was pristine but for the twin slashes in Sam's wake. Trees were bent in the wind, snow drifting from heavy branches. She could almost hear his laughter, echoing in her memory. But, she thought as a stranger lifted the photo off its display board, that was then— this was now.

"I remember that day."

Sam's voice came from right behind her and Lacy was jolted out of her thoughts. She turned to look at him, but he was watching the photograph the older man carried.

"Jack was in Germany and it was just you and me on the slopes."

"I remember." She stared up at him and saw the dreaminess in his green eyes. Caught up in the past, she followed him down Memory Lane.

"Do you also remember how that day ended?" He ran one hand down the length of her arm, giving her a chill that was filled with the promise of heat.

"Of course I do."

As if she could ever forget. They'd made love in the ski-lift cabin as snow fell and wiped away the tracks they'd left on the mountain. She remembered feeling as though they were the only two people in the world, caught up in the still silence of the falling snow and the wonder of Sam loving her.

It had all been so easy back then. She loved Sam. Sam loved her. And the future had spread out in front of them with a shining glory. Then two years later, Jack was dead, Sam was gone and Lacy was alone.

Now he was watching her with warmth in his eyes and a half smile on his lips, and Lacy felt her heart take a tumble she wasn't prepared to accept. Love was so close she could almost touch it. Fear was there, too, though. So she pushed memories into the back of her mind.

"What are you doing at a craft fair?" she blurted out.

He shrugged. "Kristi told Tony where the two of you would be, so we decided to come down and meet up. Thought maybe we could join you for lunch."

Just the thought of lunch made her stomach churn enough that even her popped corn wasn't going to help. She swallowed hard and breathed deeply through her nose. Honestly, she was praying this was something simple. Like the plague.

"Hey." He took her arm in a firm grip. "Are you okay? You just went as pale as the snow in your pictures."

"I'm fine," she said, willing herself to believe it. "Just an upset stomach, I think."

He stared at her, his gaze delving into hers as if he could pry all her secrets loose. Lacy met his gaze, refusing to look away and give him even more reason to speculate. "You're sure that's the problem?"

He was thinking *baby*, just as she was. But since she didn't have the answer to his question, she sidestepped it. "I'm sure. Just not very hungry is all."

"Okay…" He didn't look convinced, but at least he was willing to stop staring at her as if she were a bomb about to explode. Glancing back at the prints being displayed in the booth, he said, "Your photography's changed as much as you have."

"What does that mean?"

He shifted his gaze back to her, then reached out and helped himself to some of her popcorn. "You've grown. So have your photos. There's more depth. More—" he looked directly into her eyes "—layers."

Lacy flushed a little under the praise and was more touched than she was comfortable admitting. Over the past two years, she *had* changed. She'd been forced to grow up, to realize that though she had loved Sam, she could survive without him. She could have a life she loved, was proud of, without him. And though the empty space in her heart had remained, she'd become someone she was proud of. Knowing that he saw, recognized and even liked those changes was disconcerting. To cover up the rush of mixed feelings, she asked, "Is that a backhanded compliment?"

"No," he said with a shake of his head. "Nothing backhanded about it. Just an observation that you're a hell of a woman."

He was looking at her as if he was really *seeing* her—all of her—and she read admiration in his eyes. That was a surprise, and damned if she didn't like it.

A little too much. He was getting to her in a big way. What she was beginning to feel for Sam Wyatt now was so much more than she'd once felt and that worried her. When he left before, she'd survived it, but she didn't know if she could do that again.

"Well, I should look for Kristi—"

"Oh, she left with Tony," Sam told her with a half smile that made him look so approachable, so like the Sam she used to know that it threw her for a second. The then and now blended together and became a wild mix of *throwing Lacy for a loop*. When his words finally clicked in, though, she said, "Wait. She left?"

"He offered to buy her a calzone at La Ferrovia."

"Ah." Lacy nodded, understanding why her best friend had ditched her for her boyfriend. "He does know her weak spots. But who can blame her? Those calzones are legendary."

"Yeah," he said, and started walking alongside her as she turned to move down the crowded aisle. "When I was in Italy, I tried to find one as good as their spinach-cheese calzone and couldn't do it."

"Italy, huh?" Her heart tugged a little, thinking about the time he was away from her. What he'd done, seen. And yes, fine, who he'd been with. She shouldn't care. He'd left her, after all. But it was hard to simply shut down your own feelings just because someone else had tossed them in your face.

"It was beautiful," he said, but he didn't look pleased with whatever memories were rising. "Jack always loved Italy."

"Did you?"

He took more of the popcorn and munched on it. "It was nice. Parts of it were amazing. But seeing something great when you're on your own isn't all that satisfying, as it turns out." He shrugged. "There's no one to turn to and say, *isn't that something*? Still, it was good to be there. See it the way Jack did. But I never did find a calzone as good as La Ferrovia's."

An answer that wasn't an answer, Lacy thought, and wondered why he was bothering to be so ambiguous. She would have thought that he'd love seeing the top skiing spots in Europe. The fact that he clearly hadn't, made her wonder. And she hated that she cared.

"But you're happy to make do now with my popcorn," she said.

"And the company," he added, dipping one hand into the bag again. "This stuff is great, by the way."

"Chelsea Haven makes it, sells it at all the craft fairs and at one of the shops on Twenty-Fifth." She took another handful and added, "I got plain today because, you know. Stomach trouble."

His eyebrows lifted, but she ignored it.

"She's got lots of great flavors, too. Nacho, spicy and—my personal favorite—churro."

He laughed a little. "You're a connoisseur of corn?"

"I try," she said with a shrug, and stopped at the next booth. Wooden shelves and a display table held colorful, carefully wrapped bars of handmade soaps. From bright blue to a cool green, the soaps were labeled with their scents and the list of organic ingredients. Lacy picked up two pale blue bars and held on to them until she could pay for all of her purchases at once at the exit.

Sam studied the display for a long moment before he picked up a square of green soap, sniffed and asked, "Who makes all of this stuff?"

"A small company in Logan. I love it."

She sniffed at the bar of soap, smiled, then held it up for him to take a whiff.

"It's you," he said, giving her a soft smile. "The scent that's always clinging to your skin." He thought about it a moment, then said, "Lilac."

"Good nose," she told him, and started walking again.

"Some things a man's not likely to forget." He bent his head to hers, lowered his voice and whispered, "Like the scent of the woman he's inside of. That kind of thing is imprinted onto your memory."

She quivered from head to toe and, judging by his smile, he approved of her reaction. Her body was tingling, her brain was just a little fuzzed out and breathing seemed like such a chore. When she looked into his eyes and saw the heat there, Lacy felt her heart take another tumble, and this time she didn't try to deny it. To stop it.

When it came to Sam, there was no stopping how her body, her soul, reacted. Her brain was something else, though. She could still give herself a poke and remind herself of the danger of taking another plunge with Sam Wyatt. And yet, despite the danger, she knew there was nothing else she'd rather do. Which meant she was in very big trouble.

Then he straightened, scanned the crowd surrounding them and muttered, "I feel sort of outnumbered around here. Can't be more than a handful of men in the whole building."

"Gonna leave?" she asked, shooting him a quick look.

He met her gaze squarely. "I'm not going anywhere."

And suddenly, she knew he was talking about more than just the craft fair.

Sam stayed with her for another hour as they cruised through a craft fair that normally he wouldn't have been caught dead in. But being with Lacy on neutral ground made up for the fact that he felt a little out of place in what was generally considered female territory.

But while they walked and Lacy shopped, his mind turned over ideas. He carried her purchases in a cloth bag she'd brought with her for that purpose, and together they stepped out of the train station. Sam paused to look up, to the end of Historic Twenty-Fifth and beyond to the snow-covered mountain range in the distance. Trees were budding, the air was warmer and the sun shone down, as if designed to highlight the place in a golden glow.

"I missed this," he said, more to himself than Lacy. "I don't think I even knew how *much* I missed it until I was home again." The wind kicked up as if reminding everyone that spring was around the corner but winter hadn't really left just yet.

"Are you?" she asked, and Sam turned his head to look down at her. That long, silky braid of blond hair fell across one shoulder and loosened tendrils flew around her face, catching on her eyelashes as she watched him. "Are you home?"

Reaching out, Sam gently stroked the hair from her face and tucked it behind her ear. He'd wondered this himself for days. He hadn't been able to give his father a direct answer because he was still too torn. Leave? Walk away from the memories this mountain held and spend the rest of his life running from his own past? Or stand and face it all, reclaim the life—and the woman— he'd left behind?

And wasn't it just perfect now to realize that the woman he wanted owned the property he wanted? If he tried romancing her now, she'd never believe he wanted her for herself. Seemed as though fate was really enjoying itself at his expense.

He'd have to find a way around it, Sam told himself. Because he was done trying to hide from the past. It was time to set it all right. Starting now.

"Yeah, Lacy. I'm home. For good this time."

Eight

"I want to open a gift shop," Sam said, and watched as surprise had Lacy goggling at him. He'd been doing a lot of thinking since the two of them had walked through the arts-and-crafts fair the day before. Though he hadn't been tempted into buying anything himself, Sam was astute enough to realize that other people were. He figured that tourists would be just as anxious to shop for items made by local artisans.

He smiled at Lacy's confusion, then said, "Yeah, I know. Not exactly what you'd expect me to say. But I can see possibilities in everything."

"Is that right?"

"You bet." He eased down to sit on the corner of the desk in her office. "I already talked to you about using the photos you have of the lodge…"

"Yes?"

He grinned at her, enjoying having knocked her a

little off balance, and said, "It struck me when we were at that craft and art fair. There's a hell of a lot of talented people in the area."

"Sure," she said, warily.

"That's why I'm thinking gift shop. Something separate from the lodge, but clearly connected, too. Maybe between the lodge and the new addition that's going up." He nodded as the image filled his mind and he could actually envision what it would look like. "I'd want to have some refrigerated snacks in there, too. For people who are hungry but don't really want a full meal. Like prepackaged sandwiches, drinks, fruit, that kind of stuff…"

"Okay, that's a good idea, but—"

"But more than a snack shop—I want to display local artists. Not just your stuff, which is great, but like the wood-carver at the fair, the glass artist I saw there. I'll still want your postcards and we can sell framed prints, too."

"I don't know what to say."

Shaking his head, he said, "Knowing you, that won't last long. But my point is, if we're expanding Snow Vista, we could bring a lot of the local artists along with us for the ride. I think the tourists would love it and it would give the artists another outlet beyond the fairs to sell their stuff."

"I'm sure they'd love that," she said slowly, cautiously.

That was fine. He could deal with her suspicion. She'd see soon enough that he meant what he was saying. "We'll have a lawyer draw up agreements, of course. Specific to each artisan and what they sell."

"Agreements."

He nodded. "I'm thinking a seventy-thirty split with everyone, same as you and I will have."

"That's amazing," she said, tipping her head to one side and looking up at him as if she'd never seen him before.

"Okay, I know what you're thinking," he said. "I've never really involved myself in anything beyond the lodge or skiing itself."

"Yeah…"

"Like I told you before. People change." He shrugged and mentally brushed off whatever else might be running through Lacy's mind. "Back to the financial aspect, I think what we'll offer is fair. And we'll do well by each other, the lodge and the artists." His gaze met hers. "I want a range of different products in this shop. I want to showcase local talent, Lacy. Everyone from the artists to the chefs, to the woman who makes the blackberry preserves we use at the restaurant."

"Beth Howell."

"Right." He grabbed a piece of paper off the desk and scribbled down the name. "You know her, right? Hell, you probably know all of the artists around here."

"Most, sure…"

"That's great—then as resort manager you can be point on this. Talk to them. See what they think. When it gets closer to opening time, we'll set down the deals in legalese."

She blinked at him. "You want me to take charge of this?"

"Is that a problem?" He smiled, knowing that he'd caught her off guard again.

"No," she said quickly with a shake of her head. "I'm just surprised is all."

"Why?" He came off the desk and stood in front

of her before leaning down, bracing his hands on the arms of her chair. "You know your photos are great. Why would you be surprised that I'd want to showcase them, help you sell them?"

She blew out a breath and fiddled nervously with the end of her blond braid. "I suppose, because of our past, I wonder why you're being so...nice."

"I want you, Lacy. That one night with you wasn't enough. Not by a long shot."

She sucked in air and a faint flush swept up her cheeks, letting him know she felt the fire still burning between them.

"I'm home to stay. That means we're going to be part of each other's lives again."

Shaking her head, she started to speak, but he cut her off. "It's more than that, though. I want to dig in, make the kind of changes that are going to put Snow Vista on the map. And mostly, I want to convince *you* that I'm here and I'm not leaving."

"Why is that so important to you? Why do you care what I think?" Her voice was whisper soft and still it tore at him.

"You don't trust me," he said, and saw the flash in her eyes that proved it. He hated that she was wary of him, but again, he could understand it. "I get that. But things are different now, Lacy. I told you I've seen how much you've changed. Well, I've changed, too." He reached out and captured her nervous fingers in his. "I'm not the same man I was when I left here two years ago."

"And is that a good thing?" she asked quietly. "Or a bad thing?"

Leave it to this new Lacy to lay it out there so bluntly.

His mouth quirked. "I guess you'll have to discover that for yourself."

"It shouldn't matter to you what I think," she said.

"Yes, it should," he argued, and briefly looked down at her fingers, caught in his. "You more than anyone. I had a lot of time to think while I was gone."

"Yeah," she said shortly. "Me, too."

He nodded, acknowledging what she said even as he mentally kicked himself for putting her through so much pain. He hadn't been able to see anything beyond his own misery two years ago. Yet now everything looked clear enough to see that he'd set this whole situation in motion. He had to dig his way out of the very mess he'd created.

"My point is, I took some long, hard looks at my life. Choices made. Decisions. I didn't like a lot of them. Didn't much care for where those decisions had taken me. So now I'm home and I'm going to live with whatever it was that brought me back here."

She took a breath when he rubbed his thumb across her knuckles and he felt the soft whoosh of heat simmering into life between them. Her summer-blue eyes narrowed in caution. He understood why she was looking at him as if expecting him to turn and bolt for the door. But he was done looking for escape. He was here to stay now and she had to get used to it.

"I understand your suspicion," he said, capturing her gaze with his and willing her to not look away. "But I'm home now, Lacy. I'm not leaving again and you're gonna have to find a way to deal." He leaned in closer. "I left two years ago—"

She took a breath. "You keep reminding me of that, and trust me, it's not necessary."

"The point is, those two years changed us both—but

nothing can change what's still between us and I'm not going to let you deny that fire."

She licked her lips, clearly uneasy, and that slight action shot a jolt of heat right to his groin.

"Sam—"

Oh, yeah. She felt it. She was just determined to fight it. Well hell, he'd always liked a challenge. "I'm going to *romance* you, Lacy."

"What? Why?" She pulled her fingers from his grasp, but he saw her rubbing her fingertips as if they were still buzzing with sensation.

"Because I want you," he said simply. He wasn't going to use the *L* word—not only because she wouldn't want to hear it, but because he didn't know if he could say it again. He'd had that love once before but it hadn't held him. He wasn't ready to try and fail again. Failure simply wasn't an option, to quote some old movie. So he was going to keep this simple.

Looking deeply into her eyes, he added, "It's not just what I want, Lacy. You want me, too."

She looked as if she wanted to argue, but she didn't, and Sam called that a win. At least she was admitting, if only to herself, that the burn between them was hotter than ever.

"You're really trying to keep me off balance, aren't you?" she asked.

He gave her a slow, wicked smile. "How'm I doing?"

"Too well."

"Glad to hear it." He stood up abruptly and announced, "I'm headed over to the architect's office. I want to talk to her about designing this gift shop."

"You've already got so much going on…"

"No point in wasting time, is there?" And he meant

both the building and what lay between them. He was sure she understood that, too.

"I suppose not."

"So, talk to a few of your friends," he said, heading for the door. "See if they'd be interested in being involved."

"I'm sure they will…"

"Good," Sam said, interrupting her as he opened the office door. "We can have dinner later and talk about everything."

He took one last look at her and was pleased to see she looked completely shaken. That's how he wanted her. A little unsteady, a little unsure. If he kept her dancing on that fine edge, she'd be less likely to pull back, to cling to her anger. Sam was determined that he would find a way back into her life. To have her in his. And he knew just the way to do it.

Back in the day, he hadn't given Lacy romance. They'd simply fallen into love and then into marriage, and it had all been so easy. Maybe, he thought as he stalked through the lobby and out the front door, that was why it had fallen apart. It was all so easy he hadn't truly appreciated what he'd had until he'd thrown it away.

He wasn't going to make that mistake again.

Two hours later, Lacy was at home, closed up in the bathroom, staring down at the counter and the three— count them, *three*—pregnancy tests.

She'd driven into Logan to buy them just so she wouldn't run into anyone she knew in the local drug-store. She'd bought three different kinds of early-response tests because she was feeling a little obsessive and didn't really trust results to just one single test. And for the first time in her life, she got straight A's on three separate tests.

Positive.

All three of them.

Lacy lifted her gaze to her own reflection in the bathroom mirror. She waited for a sense of panic to erupt inside her. Waited to see worry shining in her own eyes. But those emotions didn't come. Her mind raced and her heart galloped just to keep pace.

"Oh, my God. Really?" Her voice echoed in the quiet cabin. All alone, she took a moment to smile and watched herself as the smile became a grin. She was going to have a baby.

Instinctively, she dropped one hand to lay it gently against her abdomen as if comforting the child within. When she and Sam were together, she had daydreamed about building a family with him. About how she might tell him the happy news when she got pregnant.

"Times change," she muttered. "Now it's not *how* to tell him, but *if* to tell him."

She had to, though, didn't she? Sure she did. That was just one of the rules people lived by. They'd made a baby together and he had a right to know. "Oh, boy, not looking forward to that."

Funny, a couple of years ago, there would have been celebration, happiness. Now she was happy. But what about Sam? He said he wanted her, but that wasn't love. Lust burned bright but went to ash just as quickly. And love was no guarantee anyway. He had loved her two years ago, but he'd left anyway. She loved him now, but it wasn't enough.

"Oh, God." She stared into her own eyes and watched them widen with realization. Kristi was right. Lacy *did* still love Sam. But that love had changed, just as she had. It was bigger. More grown-up. Less naive. She knew there were problems. Knew she wasn't on steady ground, and it wasn't enough to wipe away what she felt. Especially when she didn't know if she *wanted* it wiped away. God, she really was a glutton for punishment. Just pitiful.

The baby added another layer to this whole situation. Yes, Sam had to know.

"But," she told the girl in the mirror, "none of the rules say *when* you have to tell him."

The problem was, she wanted him to be here right now. Wanted to turn into his arms and feel them come around her. She wanted to share this…magic with him and see him happy about it. She wanted him to love her.

Stepping away from the counter, she plopped down onto the closed toilet seat and just sat there in stunned silence. She was still in love with the man who had once shattered her heart. She might have buried her emotions and her pain for two long years, but she hadn't been able to completely cut him out of her heart. He had stayed there because he belonged there, Lacy thought. He always had.

But loving him was a one-way ticket to misery if he didn't love her back. And if she told him about the baby, he'd say and do all the right things—she knew him well enough to know that for certain. He'd want to get married again maybe. Raise their child together, and she would never really know if he would have chosen *her* without the baby. Would he have come not just back home, but back to *her*?

She couldn't live an entire life never knowing, never sure.

Slowly, she pushed to her feet, stared at the test kits, then swept all three of them into the trash can. Patting her abdomen, she said, "No offense, sweetie, but I need to know if your daddy would want me even if you weren't here. So let's keep this between us for a while, okay?"

"You all right?" Sam asked the next morning when he caught her staring off into space. "Still have an upset stomach?"

"What?" Lacy jolted a little. "Um, no. Feel much better." Not a lie at all, she told herself. Once she got past the first fifteen or twenty minutes of feeling like death, everything really lightened up. Of course, she really missed coffee. Herbal tea was just…disappointing.

"Okay." He gave her a wary look as if trying to decide if she was telling the truth or not. "You were acting a little off last night when I stopped by your place with dinner, too."

Because she had still been reeling with the shock of finding herself pregnant. She hadn't really expected him to show up, especially bringing calzones from La Ferrovia. And once he was in the cabin, she had assumed that he would make a move to get her back into bed. But he hadn't. Instead, they'd talked about old times, his new plans for the resort, everything in fact, except what was simmering between them.

For a couple of hours, they'd shared dinner, laughter and a history that was made up of a lifetime of knowing each other. And darn it, Lacy thought, she had been completely charmed and thrown off balance again. He'd said he was going to give her romance, and if last night was the beginning of that, he was off to a great start.

"Have you had a chance to talk to any of your friends about the gift shop?"

"Oh, I did get a couple of them on the phone and

they're very interested." Excited, actually. Thrilled to be asked and to have another venue to sell their wares.

"Good." He shoved both hands in his pockets and stared out the office window at the view. "I'm meeting with the architect in an hour. I want the plans drawn up as soon as possible."

"I don't think that'll be a problem," she said wryly.

He glanced at her. "Why's that?"

"Nobody says no to you for long, do they?"

Sam's mouth quirked. "That include you?"

She felt her balance dissolving beneath her feet. One smile from him, one whispered comment sent jagged shards of heat slicing through her. It just wasn't fair that he had so much ammunition to use against her.

Rather than let him see that he was getting to her, Lacy replied, "As I recall, I also said 'yes' a couple of weeks ago."

"Yeah," he said, gaze moving over her like a touch. "You did."

She squirmed in her chair, then forced herself to settle when she noticed him noticing.

"Don't get jumpy," he said, coming around the desk to lean over her.

"If you don't want me jumpy, you should back up a little."

That smile came again. "Seduction in the office isn't romance, so you're safe from me at the moment."

It could be, she thought wistfully. Lock the door, draw the blinds and—oh, yeah, the office could work. Oh, boy.

He kissed her light and quick, then straightened up. "I'm heading into Ogden to the meeting with the architect. If you need me, you've got my cell number."

"Yeah. I do." *If you need me.* She smothered a sigh. She did need him, but probably not in the way he meant.

"Okay then."

He was almost at the door when she remembered something she had to run by him. "I hired an extra chef to give Maria some help in the kitchen. He starts tomorrow."

"That works," he said, and gave her a long look. "You don't have to run this stuff by me, Lacy. You've done a hell of a job managing the resort for a long time now. I trust you."

Then he left and Lacy was alone with those three words repeating in her mind. *He trusted her.*

And she was keeping his child a secret from him. Was she wrong to wait? To see if maybe his idea to romance her had more to do with reigniting love rather than the flash and burn of desire?

How could she know? All she had to go on were her instincts and they were screaming at her to protect herself—because if he shattered her again, she might not be able to pick up all the pieces this time.

For the next few weeks, Sam concentrated on setting his plans into motion. As February became March and spring crept closer day by day, he was busier than ever. It felt good, digging back into Snow Vista, making a new place for himself here. And Lacy was a big part of that. They had dinner together nearly every night—he'd taken to showing up at the cabin bringing burgers or Italian or Chinese. They talked and planned, and though it was killing him not to, he hadn't tried to smooth her into bed again yet.

He was determined to give her the romance neither of them had had the first time around. And that included sending her flowers, both at work and at her house. The wariness in her eyes was fading and he was glad to see it go.

A roaring engine from one of the earth movers working on the restaurant site tore through his thoughts and brought him back to the moment. The construction team was digging out and leveling the ground for the foundation. As long as the sun kept shining and temperatures stayed above freezing, they'd be getting the lodge addition started by next week. The hard-core, hate-to-see-winter-end skiers were still flocking to the mountain, but for most of the tourists, the beginning of spring meant the end of looking for snow.

Which brought him back to the latest plan he'd already set in motion. Right now there was an engineer and a surveying crew laying out the best possible route for his just-like-Park-City forest ride. There would be rails for individual cars and the riders would be able to slow down if they didn't like the speed attached to careening down a mountain slope. The architects were busily drawing up plans and making the changes that the Wyatt family insisted on.

Sam smiled to himself, stuffed his hands into the pockets of his battered black leather jacket and turned his face into the wind. Here at the top of Snow Vista, the view was, in his opinion, the best in the world. Damned if he hadn't missed it.

He'd been all over the planet, stood on top of the Alps, skied amazing slopes in Germany, Italy and Austria, yet this was the view that for him couldn't be beaten. The pines were tall and straight in the wind, and the bare branches of the oaks and aspens chattered like old women gossiping. Soon, the trees would green up, the wildflowers would be back and the river through the canyon would run fresh and clear again.

His gaze swept across the heavily wooded slope that was unusable for skiing. The alpine ride he wanted installed would make great use of that piece of land. Like a roller coaster but without the crazy dips and climbs. It would be a slower, open-air ride through the trees, displaying the fantastic views available from the top of the mountain. Like Park City, Snow Vista could become known for summer as well as winter fun.

He could see it all. The lifts, the alpine coaster, the restaurant offering great food at reasonable prices. Hell, Sam told himself, as he turned to shift his view to the meadow, still blanketed in snow, with a gazebo and a few other additions, they could open the resort to weddings, corporate getaways…the possibilities were endless.

And he'd be here, to see it all. He waited for the urge to leave and when it didn't come, he smiled. It really was good to be back.

"I know the sun's out, but it's still too cold to be standing around outside."

Chuckling, Sam turned to face his sister.

"It's spring, Kristi," Sam said. "Enjoy the cool before the summer heat arrives."

She walked toward him, her hair pulled back from her face, a black jacket pulled over a red sweater and jeans. As she approached, her features were as cool as the wind sliding across the mountain. His little sister hadn't really said anything about his decision to stay and Sam knew that she and Lacy were the ones he'd have to work hardest to convince. He was pretty sure he had Lacy halfway there, but maybe now was his chance to get through to his sister.

"You haven't even been back a full month and you've

got the whole mountain running to catch up with your ideas."

Sam shrugged. "Now that I've decided to stay, there's no point in holding back." He looked away from Kristi and sent a sharp-eyed look at the men working the half-frozen ground. "I want the resort to be up and offering new things as quickly as possible."

"Hence the bonus money offered the crew if they get both foundations poured before April 1?"

Sam grinned. "Money's a great motivator."

"It is," she acknowledged. "And Dad's really happy with everything you're doing."

"I know." It felt good, knowing that his father was excited about the future. That meant he was thinking ahead, not about the past or about his own health issues. Sam was still stopping in at the lodge every day to go over the plans with his father. To keep the older man engaged in what was going on. To get his input and, hell—just to be with him. Sam had missed that connection with his parents over the past two years. Being here with them again was good for the soul— even with the ghost of Jack hanging over all of them, whether he was spoken of or not. But even with that, with the memories of sorrow clinging close, even with the complications nearly choking him, it was good to be on familiar ground again.

"What about you, Kristi?" His gaze shifted to her again. "How are you feeling about all of this? About me?"

She took a breath and let it out. "I like all of the plans," she said, lifting her eyes to meet his. "But the jury's still out on what I'm thinking of you."

Sam felt his good mood drift away and decided that now was the time to get a few things straightened out with his little sister. "How long are you going to make me pay?"

"How long have you got?" Kristi shrugged, but her eyes were clouded with emotion rather than anger.

"I can't keep saying I'm sorry." Apologizing had never come easy for Sam. Not even when he was a kid. Having to swallow the fact that he'd screwed up royally two years ago wasn't exactly a walk in the park. But he was doing it.

"I came back," he told her. "That has to count, too."

"Maybe it does, because I am glad you're back, Sam. Really." She shoved both hands into her jacket pockets and tossed a strand of hair out of her eyes with a single jerk of her head. "You being here is a good thing. But what you did two years ago affected all of us and that's not so easy to get past."

"Yeah, I know." He nodded grimly, accepting the burden of past decisions. "Lacy. Mom. Dad."

"Me," she snapped out, and stepped up close enough to him that the toes of their boots collided. Tipping her head back, she glared up at him, her eyes suddenly alive with anger, and said, "You leaving taught me that trusting *anyone* was too risky. Did you know Tony's asked me to marry him twice now and twice I told him no?"

He inhaled sharply. "No, I didn't know that."

"Well, he did. And I said no because—" her voice broke off, she swallowed hard and pinned him with a hot look designed to singe his hair. "Because if *you* could leave Lacy, how could I possibly trust that Tony would stay with me? What's the point, right? I couldn't make myself believe, because you ripped the rug out from under me."

"Damn it, Kristi." Talk about feeling lower than he would have thought possible. Somehow in screwing over his own life, he'd managed to do the same for his baby sister. One more piece of guilt to add to the burden he already carried. Sam gritted his teeth and accepted it. Then he dropped both hands onto her shoulders and held on.

"You can't use me as an excuse for not trying. I messed things up pretty well, but they were *my* decisions." Bitter pill to choke down, but there it was. "You can't judge everyone else by what I did. Tony's a great guy and you know it. You're in charge of your own life, Kristi. Make it or break it on your own. Just like the rest of us."

"Easy to say when you're not the one left behind."

She had a point, though it cut at him to admit it. Damn, the repercussions of what he'd done two years ago just kept coming. It was like dropping a damn rock into a pond and watching the ripples spread and reach toward shore. But even as he acknowledged that, he tried to cut himself a break, too.

When Jack died, Sam hadn't been able to think. Hadn't been able to take a breath through his own pain, and he'd reacted to that. Escaping the memories, the people, who were all turning to him for answers he didn't have. The emptiness he'd felt at his brother's death had driven him beyond logic, beyond reason. Now, his decision to come home again meant he was forced to face the consequences of his actions. Acknowledging the pain he'd dealt others was hard to swallow.

He looked at Kristi and saw her in flashing images through his mind at every stage of her life. The baby his parents had brought home from the hospital. The tiny blonde girl chasing after him and Jack. The prom date Jack and he had tortured with promises of pain if he got out of line with their sister. The three siblings laughing together at the top of the mountain before hurtling down the slope in one of the many races they'd indulged in. Slowly, though, the memories faded and he was looking into her eyes, seeing the here and now, and love for her filled him.

Going with instinct, he pulled her, resisting, in for a hug, and rested his chin on top of her head. It only took a second or two for her to wrap her arms around his waist and hold on. "Damn it Sam, we needed you—I needed you—and you weren't here."

"I am now," he said, waiting until she looked up at him again. She was beautiful and sad, but no longer furious and he was silently grateful that the two of them had managed to cross a bridge to each other. "But, Kristi, don't let my mistakes make you miss something amazing. You love Tony, right?"

"Yes, but—"

"No." He cut her off with a shake of his head. "No buts. You've always been nuts about him and it's clear he loves you, too, or he wouldn't put up with all of those self-help books you're always quoting."

She snorted and dipped her head briefly. The smile was still curving her mouth when she looked up at him again.

Shaking his head, Sam said softly, "Don't use me as an excuse for playing it safe, Kristi. Nobody's perfect, kid. Sometimes, you have to take a chance to get something you want."

She scowled at him, then chewed at her bottom lip.

He smiled and planted a kiss on her forehead. "Trust Tony. Hell, Kristi, trust *yourself.*"

"I'll try," she said, then added, "I'm so glad you're home."

"Me, too, kid. Me, too."

Nine

The talk with his sister was still resonating with him when Sam stopped at Lacy's cabin later that night. For hours, he'd heard Kristi's voice repeating in his mind as he came to grips with what he'd put everyone through two years ago. Realizing what he'd cost himself had brought him to the realization that he not only wanted but *needed* Lacy in his life again. Now he had to find a way to make that happen.

The occasional night with her wasn't enough. He wanted more. And Sam wasn't going to stop until he had it.

He brought pizza and that need to be with her. To just be in the same damn room with her. To be able to look into those eyes that had haunted him for too long and realize he had a second chance to make things right.

"Bringing a pizza is cheating," Lacy told him, settling back into the couch with a slice of that pizza on a stoneware plate.

He laughed. "How? Gotta eat. You always loved pizza."

"Please." She rolled her eyes and shook her head. "Everyone loves pizza."

"Not many people love it with pepperoni and pineapple."

She took a bite and gave a soft groan of pleasure that had his body tightening in response. "Peasants who don't know what's good," she said with a shrug.

Ordinarily he might enjoy bantering with her, but tonight, he couldn't seem to settle. Sam set his pizza aside and looked into the fire that burned cheerily in the hearth. The hiss and crackle of flames was a soothing sound, but it did nothing for the edginess he felt. He couldn't shake that conversation with Kristi.

"What's wrong?"

He looked at her, firelight dancing across her face, highlighting the gold of her hair lying loose across her shoulders. That same flickering light glittered in her eyes as she watched him. She wore jeans, a deep red sweater and a pair of striped socks, and still, she was the most beautiful woman he'd ever seen.

"Sam? What is it?"

He got to his feet, stalked to the fireplace and planted both hands on the mantel as he stared into the flames. "I talked to Kristi today."

"I know. She told me."

Of course she had. Women told each other everything—a fact that gave most men cold chills just to think about it. He turned to look at her. "Did she tell you that she's been putting her whole damn life on pause because of what I did two years ago?"

"Yeah, she did."

He pushed one hand through his hair, turned his back

on the fire and faced her dead on. His brain was racing; guilt raked his guts with sharpened claws. "I never
realized, you know, how much my decisions two years
ago affected everyone else."

Lacy set her pizza aside and folded her hands in her
lap as she looked at him. "How could they not, Sam?"

Scrubbing the back of his neck, he blurted, "Yeah, I
see that now. But back then, I couldn't see past my own
pain. My own misery."

"You wouldn't let any of us help. You shut us all
out, Sam."

"I know that," he said tightly. "I do. But I couldn't
reach out to you, Lacy. Not when the guilt was eating
me alive."

"Why should you feel guilty about what happened
to Jack? I don't understand that at all."

He blew out a breath, swallowed hard and admitted,
"When Jack first got sick—diagnosed with leukemia—
that's when the guilt started."

"Sam, why? You didn't make him sick."

He choked out a sharp laugh. "No, I didn't. But I was
healthy and that was enough. We were *identical twins*,
Lacy. The same damn egg made us both. So why was
he sick and I wasn't? Jack never said it, but I know he
was thinking it because I was. Why him? Why not me?"

A soft sigh escaped her and he didn't know if it was
sympathy or frustration.

Didn't matter now anyway. He was finally telling
her exactly what had been going through his head back
then, and he had to get it finished. But damn, it was
harder than he would have thought. Shaking his head,
he reached up to scrub one hand across the back of his
neck and started talking again.

"I was with Jack through the whole thing, but I

couldn't share it. Couldn't take my half of it and make it easier on him." His hand fisted and he thumped it uselessly against his side as his mind took him back to the darkest days of his life. "I felt so damn helpless, Lacy. I couldn't *do* anything."

"You did do something, though, Sam," she reminded him. "You gave him bone marrow. You gave him a chance and it worked."

He snorted at the reminder of how high their hopes had been. Of the relief Sam had felt for finally being able to help his twin. To save his life. "For all the good it did in the end."

"I never knew you were feeling all of this." She stood up, walked to him and looked into his eyes. "Why didn't you talk to me about this then, Sam?"

He blew out a breath. Meeting her eyes was the hardest thing he'd ever done. Trying to explain the unexplainable was just as difficult. "How could I tell my wife that I felt guilty for being married? Happy? Alive?" He pushed both hands through his hair, then sucked in air like a drowning man hoping for a few more seconds of life before the sea dragged him down. "God, Lacy, you were loving me and Jack had no one."

"He had *all* of us," she countered.

"You know what I mean." He shook his head again. "He was *dying* right in front of me."

"Us."

She was right, he knew. Jack's loss was bigger than how it had affected Sam. He could remember his parents' agony and worry. The whispered prayers in the mint-green, soulless, hospital waiting room. He saw his father age and watched his mother hold back tears torn from her heart and still... "I couldn't feel that then," he admitted. "*Wouldn't* feel it. I was watching my twin die and I was so messed up I couldn't see a way out."

"But you finally found one…"

"Yeah," he said softly, looking into those eyes of hers, seeing the sorrow, the regret, and hating himself for causing it then and reawakening it now. "I don't know if you can understand what I did, Lacy. Hell, I don't even know if I do, now."

"Try me." She folded her arms across her chest and waited.

God, two years he'd been holding everything inside him. Letting it all out was like—he couldn't even think of the right metaphor. It was damned painful but it was long past time he told Lacy exactly what had happened then. Why he'd done what he'd done.

"After the bone-marrow transplant, after it worked and Jack was in remission, it was like…" He paused, looking for the right words, and was sure he wouldn't be able to find them. Not to explain what he had felt. Finally, he just started talking again and hoped for the best. "It was like fate had suddenly said, 'Okay, Sam. You can go ahead and be happy again. Your brother's alive. You saved him. So everything's good.'"

He could remember it so well, the nearly crippling relief, the laughter. Watching his brother recover, get strong again, believing that their world was righting itself.

Lacy reached out and gently laid one hand on his forearm. It felt like a damn lifeline to Sam, holding him to this place, this time, not letting him go too deeply into a past filled with misery. He covered her hand with his, needing that warmth she offered him as he finished.

Sam looked down at their joined hands and said softly, "Jack was full of plans, Lacy. He was well again, and after so long feeling like crap, he couldn't wait to get back out into the world."

"I remember," she said quietly.

The snap and hiss of the flames was the only sound in the room for a few seconds. "He showed me his 'list.' Not a bucket list, since he wasn't dying anymore. It was a dream list. A *life* list. His first stop was going to be Germany. Staying with some friends while he skied the slopes and reclaimed everything the cancer stole from him."

She didn't speak, just kept looking at him through eyes gleaming with the shine of tears she wouldn't allow to fall.

"He was well, damn it." Sam pulled away from her and scrubbed both hands over his face like a man trying to wake up from a nightmare. "Jack was happy again and on the road and then he *dies* in a damn car wreck on the freeway? It was crazy. Surreal."

"I know, Sam. I was with you. We all were."

"That's the thing, Lacy." His gaze caught hers again as he willed her to understand how it had been for him. "You were there but I couldn't have you. Couldn't *let* myself have you because Jack was dead and his dreams with him. I *saved* him and he died anyway. It was like fate was screwing with us just for the hell of it. None of it made sense. I couldn't bring him back. So I told myself I had to do the next best thing. I had to at least keep his dreams alive."

Seconds ticked past before Lacy stared up at him and said, "That's why you left? To pick up the list Jack left behind and make it happen?"

"He had all these plans. Big ones. And with him gone, those plans were all I had left of him. How could I let them die, too?"

"Sam—" She broke off, took a breath and said, "Did you really think fulfilling Jack's list was going to keep him with you?"

God, why did it sound stupid when she said it? It hadn't been at the time. But that's exactly what he'd thought. By living his twin's dreams, in essence, his twin's *life*, it would be as if Jack never died.

"It was important to me," he muttered thickly. "I had to keep him alive somehow."

"God, Sam..." She lifted one hand to cover her mouth and her beautiful eyes shone with tears.

"Keeping Jack with me meant distancing myself from the reality of his death. That's why I had to leave. I couldn't be here, facing the fact, every day, that he was gone."

God, he felt so stupid. So damn weak somehow for having to give up his own life because he'd been unable to accept his twin's death. He rubbed one hand across his mouth, then said, "I took Jack's dreams and lived them for him. For a while, I lost myself in ski slopes, strangers and enough alcohol to sink a ship." He snorted ruefully as memories of empty hotel rooms and staggering hangovers rose up to taunt him. "But drinking only made the pain more miserable and even skiing and being anonymous got old fast."

"You should have talked to me, Sam."

"And said what?" he asked, suddenly weary to his bones. His gaze locked on hers and everything in him wished that they were still what they had once been to each other. It rocked him a little to realize just how much he wanted her back. How much he still loved her. "What could I possibly have told you, Lacy? That I wasn't allowed to be happy because Jack was dead? You couldn't have understood."

"You're right," she said, nodding. "I wouldn't have. I'd have told you that *living* was the best way to honor Jack. Living your own dreams. Not his."

He sighed. She was right and he could see that now. He wouldn't have then. "My dreams didn't seem to matter to me once his were over."

"Did it help?" she asked quietly. "Leaving. Did it help?"

"For a while." His mouth quirked briefly. "But not for long. I couldn't find satisfaction in Jack's dreams because they weren't mine. But I owed it to him to try."

She reached up to cup his face in her palms and the soft warmth of her touch slid deep inside to ease away the last of the chill crouched in his heart. God, how had he lived for two years without her touch? Without the sound of her voice or the soft curve of her mouth? How had he been able to stay away from the one woman in the world who made his life worth living?

"Sam," she said quietly, "you don't owe Jack your life."

"I know," he said, covering her hands with his. It was too early to tell her he loved her. Why the hell should she believe him after what he'd done to their lives? Their marriage? No, he'd sneak up on her. Be a part of her world every day, slowly letting her see that he was here to stay and that he would never leave her again. "That's why I'm back, Lacy. To rebuild my life. And I want that life to include you."

"Sam…"

"Don't say anything yet, Lacy," he told her. "Just let me prove to you that I can be the man for you."

Her breath hitched and her eyes went shiny with emotion.

"Let's just take our time and discover each other again, okay?"

She nodded slowly, and in her eyes he read hope mingled with caution. Couldn't blame her for it, but he silently vowed that he'd wipe away her trepidation.

"You can trust me, Lacy. I swear it."

"I want to, Sam," she whispered, "for more reasons than you know…"

"Just give me a chance." When he pulled her close, bent his head and kissed her, she leaned into him, curving her body to his, silently letting him know that she was willing to try. And that was all he could hope for. For now.

Tenderness welled up between them and in the soft, flickering firelight, they came together as if it were the first time and the shining promise that was the future was almost in reach.

Lacy was still smiling the next morning.

She felt as though she and Sam had finally created a shaky bridge between the past and present. At long last, he'd told her what had driven him to leave, and though it still hurt, she could almost understand. As sad as they'd all been when Jack died, for Sam it had to have been even more devastating. Like losing a part of himself. And she could admit, too, that she hadn't been capable of being what he needed back then. She'd been too concerned with her own insecurities.

When Jack died, all she'd been able to think was *thank God it wasn't Sam*. She'd been too young and too untried—untested—to be able to see what Sam was going through, so how could she have helped him?

Now it was as if they were both getting a second chance to do things right. She laid one hand on her belly and whispered to the child sleeping within, "I think it's going to be all right, baby. Your daddy and I are going to make it happen. Build a future in spite of the past."

And just to prove to herself—and him—that she was willing to trust him, willing to believe, she had decided to tell him about the baby that night at dinner.

Whoa. Her stomach did a quick twist and spin at the thought. Nervous, yes, but it was the right thing to do. If they were going to work this out between them and have it stick this time, she had to be as honest as he had been the night before.

She gave the baby a gentle pat, then, smiling, she headed through the lobby. There were guests sprinkled around the great room, enjoying the fire, having a snack, chatting. She ignored them all, stepped outside and took a deep breath of the chill spring air. Tulips and daffodils were spearing up, trees were beginning to green.

It was as if the snow was melting along with the ice in her heart. Lacy felt lighter than she had in two years. And she was ready to let go of the past and rush to a future that was suddenly looking very bright.

"Lacy! Hey, Lacy!"

She turned and grinned at Kevin Hambleton as he jogged toward her. Kevin was young, working his first season at the lodge. He was helping out at the ski-rental shop, but had been angling for an instructor's position.

"Hi, Kevin," she said as he started walking with her toward the ski lift that would take her to the new construction site. Not only did she want to see how the building was coming along, she could admit to herself that she wanted to see Sam, too. And she knew that if he wasn't at the lodge, working in the office, he would be at the site, watching his plans come to life. "I'm just going up to check on the guys, see what progress they're making."

"It's great, isn't it?" His face practically shone with excitement. "A lot of things happening around here now that Sam's back."

"There are, with more to come," she said, thinking about the gift shop, the portico and the expansion to the lodge. Within a couple of years, Snow Vista would be a premier tourist destination.

"I know, I read that in the paper this morning."

"What?" She looked up at him. As far as she knew, the gift shop hadn't been announced.

"Yeah, there was this article, talking about all the changes and how Sam's going to put in a new beginner's run on the back side of the mountain and all..."

Lacy shook her head, frowned and tried to focus on what he was saying. But her heart was pounding and her brain was starting to short-circuit. "He's building a run on the backside?"

"Yeah, and I wanted to put my name in with you early, you know?" He grinned. "Get in on the ground floor. I really want to be an instructor and I figured starting out with the newbies would be a good idea, you know?"

"Right." Mind racing, Lacy heard Kevin's excited voice now as nothing more than a buzz of sound. The cold wind slapped at her, people around her shouted or laughed and went about their business. It was all she could do to put one foot in front of the other.

"With a new run going in, you'll need more instructors, so I just, you know, wanted to see if maybe you'd think about me first."

He was standing there, staring at her with a hopeful

grin on his face, the freckles across his cheeks bright splashes of gold.

The edges of her vision went dark until she was looking at Kevin as if through a telescope. She felt faint, her head was light and there was a ball of ice in the pit of her stomach. Through the clanging in her brain and the wild thumping of her heart, Lacy knew she had to say *something*.

"How did you hear about the new run?"

"Like I said," he told her, his eyes a little less excited now, "I saw it in the paper. Well, my mom did and she told me."

He was looking worried now, as if he'd done something wrong, so Lacy gave him a smile and a friendly pat on the shoulder to ease him. No reason to punish him just because *her* world was suddenly rocking wildly out of control. "Okay then, Kevin. I'll put your name down."

"Thanks!" Breath whooshed out of him in relief. "A lot, really. Thanks, Lacy."

When he ran off again, she watched him go, but her mind wasn't on Kevin any longer. It was fixed solely on Sam Wyatt. The lying bastard. God. She thought about the night before—as she had been doing all morning—only now she was looking at it through clearer eyes.

And heck, it wasn't just last night, it was the past few weeks. Romancing her. She nearly choked. He'd said he was going to romance her, but that wasn't what he'd been doing. This whole time, he'd been conducting a sort of chess match, with her as the pawn, to be moved wherever he wanted her. He'd spent weeks softening her up, until he could apply the coup de grâce last night. Then he rolled her up in sympathy, let her shed a few tears for him, for them, then he'd swept her into bed, where rational thinking was simply not an option.

"Oh, he was good," she murmured, gaze fixed on the top of the mountain where she knew he was, but not really seeing it. "He actually convinced me. He had me."

And wasn't that a lowering thing to admit? Lacy cringed internally as she remembered just how easily she'd fallen for charm and lies. Sam had slipped beneath her radar and gotten past every one of her defenses. He'd made her feel *sorry* for him. Made her forgive him for what he'd done to her two years ago. Made her *believe* again. Last night, he'd convinced her at last that maybe they had a chance of rebuilding their lives.

But he wasn't really interested in that at all. Or in *her*. She was a means to an end. All he wanted from her was the land his family had given her. For his plans. For his changes. He was sweeping her aside just as he had two years ago. And just like then, she hadn't noticed until she had tire tracks on her back.

Temper leaped into life and started pawing at her soul like a bull preparing to charge. Well, she wasn't the same Lacy now. She was tougher. Stronger. She'd had to be.

And this time, he wasn't going to get away with it.

She found him at the construction site, just where she'd expected him to be. Sam spent half his time up here, talking to the men, watching the progress of the new restaurant going up. And all the while, he was probably planning his takeover of her property, too.

The ride on the ski lift hadn't calmed or soothed Lacy as it usually did. Normally, the sprawling view spreading out beneath her, the sensation of skimming through the sky was enough to ease away every jagged edge inside her. But not today. The edges were too sharp. Cutting too deeply.

The rage she'd felt when Kevin first stopped her and spilled his news had grown until it was a bubbling froth rising up from the pit of her stomach to the base of her throat. Her hands shook with the fury and her eyes narrowed dangerously against the sun glinting off what was left of the snowpack. Shaking her head, she jumped off the lift when it reached the top and before she could even *try* to cool down, she followed the steady roar of men and machines to the site.

Sam stood there, hands in the pockets of his black leather jacket, wind tossing his dark hair into a tumble and his gaze fixed on the men hustling around what looked to her like the aftermath of a bombing. He couldn't have heard her approach over the crashing noise, but as she got closer, he somehow sensed her and turned to smile. That smile lasted a fraction of a second before draining away into a puzzled frown.

"Lacy?" His voice was pitched high enough to carry over the construction noise. "Everything okay?"

"*Nothing* is okay and you know it," she countered, sprinting toward him until she was close enough to stab her index finger against his chest. "How could you do that? You lied to me. You used my own pain against me. You played me, Sam. Again."

"What the hell are you talking about?"

Oh, he was a better actor than she'd given him credit for. The expression of stunned surprise might actually have been convincing if she didn't already know the truth. "You know damn well what I'm talking about so don't bother playing innocent."

God, she was so furious she could hardly draw a breath.

But the words clogging her throat didn't have any trouble leaping out at him. "Kevin told me what's really going on around here. I should have known. Should have guessed. Romancing me," she added snidely. "Flowers. Dinner."

If anything, the confusion on his face etched deeper until Lacy wanted to just smack him. She'd never been a violent person, but at the moment she sorely wished she was.

"Why don't you calm down," he was saying. "We'll go talk and you can tell me what's bothering you?"

"Don't you tell me to calm down!" She reached up and tugged at her own hair, flying loose in the wind. "I can't believe I fell for it. I was this close—" she held up her thumb and index finger just a whisker apart "—to trusting you again. I thought last night meant something—"

Now anger replaced confusion and his features went taut as his eyes narrowed. "Last night *did* mean something."

"Sure," she countered, through the pain, the humiliation of knowing it had all been an act. "It was the cherry on top of the sundae of lies you've been building for weeks. The grand finale of the Romance Lacy Plan. My God, I went for it all, didn't I? Your sadness, your grief." She huffed in a breath, disgusted with him, with herself, with everything. "I've got to give you credit— it really did the job on me. Then slip me into bed fast and make me remember how it used to be for us. Make me *want* it."

A couple of the machines went silent and the drop in the noise level was substantial, but she kept going. She was aware of nothing beyond the man staring at her as if she were speaking in tongues.

"You set this whole thing up, didn't you? Right from the beginning."

"Set *what* up?" He threw both hands in the air and let them fall to his sides again. "If you'll tell me what you're talking about maybe I could answer that."

"The backside of the mountain," she snapped. "*My* land. The land your folks deeded to me." Her breath was hitching, her voice catching. "You want it for a new beginner run. Kevin told me he saw it in the paper this morning. Your secret's out, Sam. I know the truth now, and I'm here to tell you it's not going to work."

"The *paper*?" he repeated, clearly astonished. "How the hell did—"

"Hah!" she shouted. "Didn't mean for the word to get out so soon, huh? Wanted a little more time to sucker me in even deeper?"

"That's not what I meant—never mind. Doesn't matter."

She gasped. "You son of a bitch, of *course* it matters. It's *all* that matters. You lied to me, Sam. You used me. And damn it, I let you." She was so stupid. How could she have been foolish enough to let him get into her heart again? How could she have, even for a moment, allowed herself to hope? To dream?

"Now just wait a damn minute," Sam blurted out. "I can explain all of this."

She took a step back and didn't even notice when the last of the construction machinery cut off and silence dropped on the mountain like a stone. "Oh, I bet you can. I bet you've got stories and explanations for any contingency."

"Just a minute here, Lacy…"

"How far were you willing to go, Sam, to get what you wanted from me? Marriage?"

"If you'll just shut up and listen for a second…"

"Don't you tell me to shut up! And for your information, I'm done listening to you." She backed up a step, lifted her chin and gave him the iciest glare she could manage. "You want the land? Well you're not going to get it. The one thing you want from me, you can't have."

He moved toward her. "That's not what I want from you."

"I don't believe you." She shook her head and her gaze fixed with his. "I know the truth now. I know the real reason you've been spending so much time with me, *reconnecting*."

"You don't know anything," he said, moving in closer. "I admit, I wanted a new beginner run on the backside, but—"

"There. Finally. *Truth*." She jerked her head back as if he'd slapped her. "Did it actually hurt to say it?"

"I'm not finished."

"Oh, yes," she told him, "you are. *We* are. Whatever there was between us is done."

"It'll never be done, Lacy." His voice was dark, deep and filled with determination. "You know that as well as I do."

"What I know, is that once I believed you when you said you would never leave me. You *knew* what that meant to me. Because my own mother left me. You promised you wouldn't. You swore to love me forever." Oh, God, this was so hard. She couldn't breathe now. There were iron bands around her chest, squeezing her lungs, fisting around her heart. "And then you left. You walked away. Broke your word *and* my heart. You don't get a second chance at that. Damned if I'll bleed for you again, Sam."

"You're upset," he said, his voice carrying the faintly

patient tone that people reserved for dealing with hysterics. "When you settle down a little, we can talk this out."

She laughed and it scored her throat even as it scraped the air. "I've said what I came to say to you—and I don't want to hear another word from you. Ever."

Lacy spun around and hurried to the ski lift for a ride back down the mountain.

Sam watched her go, his own heart pounding thunderously in his chest. Silence stretched out around him, and it was only then he noticed all the men had stopped working and were watching him. They'd probably heard every word. He turned his head and caught sight of Dennis Barclay.

"Seems you're in some deep trouble there, Sam," the man said.

Truer words, he thought, but didn't let Dennis know just how worried he was. He'd never seen Lacy in a tear like that before. Even when she was furious when he first got home, even when she had yelled at him about past sins, there'd been some control. Some sort of restraint. But today there had been nothing but sheer fury and bright pain. Pain he'd caused her. Again. That thought shamed him as well as infuriated him.

How the hell had that tidbit about the beginner run made it into the paper? He hadn't told anyone. Hadn't said a word.

"She'll cool off," Dennis said, offering hope.

"Yeah," Sam agreed, though a part of him wasn't so sure. The pain and fury he'd just witnessed wasn't something that would go away quickly. If ever. Had he screwed things up so badly this time that it really was over?

Misery blossomed in his chest and wrung his heart

until the pain of it nearly brought him to his knees. A life without Lacy?

Didn't bear thinking about.

Ten

Sam's instincts told him to go to Lacy right away. Follow her. Force her to listen to him so he could straighten all this out. But his instincts two years ago had been damned wrong, so he was hesitant to listen to them now—when it mattered so much.

He denied himself the urge to go to Lacy and instead went to the lodge and upstairs to the family quarters. He wasn't even sure why, but he felt as if he needed more than being alone with the black thoughts rampaging through his mind.

The great room was empty, so he followed his nose to the kitchen. The scent of spaghetti sauce drifted to him, and in spite of everything, his stomach growled in appreciation. Another thing he'd missed while he was gone was his mother's homemade sauce. Sam stopped in the doorway and watched her at the stove while his father sat at the round oak pedestal table, laying out a hand of solitaire.

"Sam!" His father spotted him first and his mother whirled around from the stove to smile in welcome. "Good to see you," his father said. "How's the work on the mountain going? Tell me all about it since your mother won't let me go up yet."

"Everything's fine," Sam said, and walked to the table to take a seat. The kitchen was bright, cheerful, with the sunlight pouring in through windows sparkling in the light.

"You don't look too happy about it," his mother said.

He glanced at her and forced a smile. "It's not that. It's…"

"Lacy," his mother finished for him.

"Well," Sam chuckled darkly, "good to know that your mother radar is still in good shape."

Connie Wyatt grinned at her son. "It wasn't that hard to guess, but I'll take the compliment, thanks."

"So, what's going on?" his father asked as Sam sat down opposite him.

He hardly knew where to start. But hell, he'd come here to talk, to get this all off his chest. He just had to lay it all out for them, so he took a breath and blurted out, "Apparently someone talked to a reporter. It was in the paper today about me wanting to build a beginner run on Lacy's property."

"Ouch." His father winced.

"And she found out," Connie said.

"Yeah." Sam drummed his fingers on the table. "She let me have it, too. I just can't figure out how the reporter heard about it. I mean, I changed my plans when I heard the land was Lacy's."

"That's probably my fault."

"Bob," his wife demanded, "what did you do?"

Grumbling, the older Wyatt glanced first at his son,

then his wife. "A reporter called here the other day," he said, with a rueful shake of his head. "Asking questions about all the changes happening around here. Got me talking about the different runs we have to offer, then she said something about how she was a novice skier and I told her we could teach her and that you had wanted to build a brand-new beginner run on the back of the mountain, but that the plans weren't set in stone so not to say anything…and I guess she did anyway."

Sam groaned. At least that explained how it had made the paper. And, it would be a lot simpler if he could just blame this latest mess on his father. But the reality was, if Sam had just been honest with Lacy from the jump, none of this would be happening.

"Don't worry about it, Dad. She was bound to hear about it sooner or later anyway."

"Yeah, but it would've been better to hear it from you," his father pointed out.

"That ship sailed when I didn't tell her." Sam slumped back in the chair and reached for the cup of coffee his mother set in front of him. Taking a long sip, he let the heat slide through him in a welcome wave.

"So what're you going to do about all of this?" his mother asked quietly.

He looked at her. Connie was standing with her back braced against the counter, her arms folded over her chest.

"That's the thing," Sam said honestly. His chest ached like a bad tooth and he suspected his heart wasn't going to be feeling better anytime soon. Not with the way things stood between him and Lacy. "I just don't know."

And that was the truth. With Lacy's words still echoing in his mind, the wounded glint in her eyes still fresh in his memory, Sam couldn't see clearly what he should do. He knew what he *wanted* to do. Go to her. Tell her he loved her. But damned if she'd believe that *now*. It had been easier—if more selfish—two years ago, when he hadn't considered how his decision to take off would affect anyone but himself. Now, though, there was too much to think about. Just one more rock on the treacherous road his life had become.

"I almost went after her—"

"Bad idea," his father said. "Never beard a lioness in her den when she's still itching to take a bite out of you. I speak from experience," he added with a sly glance at his wife.

"Very funny," Sam's mother quipped, then turned back to Sam. "And just how long do you think it's going to take for her to cool off?"

"A decade or two ought to do it," Sam mused, only half joking. He raked one hand through his hair and sighed. "Hell, me coming home has thrown everyone off their game. Maybe it'd be best for everyone if I just left again and—"

"Don't you even say that," his mother warned, her voice cold steel. "Samuel Bennett Wyatt, don't you even *think* about leaving here again."

Shocked at the vehemence in her tone, Sam could only look at her. "I really wasn't going to leave again. I was just thinking that maybe it would be easier on everyone if I—"

"If you what?" his mother finished for him. "Disappear again? Leave us wondering if you're alive or dead again? Walk away from your home? Your family? *Again?*"

Now it was his turn to wince. Damned if Sam didn't feel the way he had at thirteen when he'd faced down his mother after driving a snowmobile into the back of the lodge.

"Mom," he said, standing up.

"No," she interrupted, pushing off the counter as if she were leaping into battle. And maybe she was. Connie took three short steps until she was right in front of her son, tipping her head back to glare at him. "Ever since you got back, I've kept my peace. I didn't say all the things I was bursting to say to you because I didn't want to rock the boat. Well, brace yourself because here it comes."

"Uh-oh," his father whispered.

His mother's eyes were swimming with tears and fury, her shoulders were tense and her voice was sharp. "When you left right after Jack died, it was like I'd lost both of my sons. You might as well have been dead, too," she continued. "You walked away, left us grieving, worrying." Planting both hands at her hips, she continued, "Four postcards in two years, Sam. That's it. It was as if you'd disappeared as completely as Jack. As if you were as out of reach as he was."

No one could make a grown man feel quite as shameful and guilt-ridden as his mother. Sam looked down at her and knew he'd never be able to make it up to her for what he'd done. "I had to go, Mom."

"Maybe," she allowed tightly with a jerking nod. "Maybe you did, but you're back now, and if you leave again, you'll be no better than Jack was, always running away from life."

"What?" Staggered, Sam argued, "No, that's wrong. Jack was all about living life to the fullest. He grabbed every ounce of pleasure he could out of every single day."

She sighed heavily and Sam watched the anger drain

from her as she shook her head and reached up to cup his cheek in her palm. "Oh, honey. Jack was all about *experiences*, not living. The fastest cars. Best skis. Highest mountain. That's not *life*. That's indulgence."

He'd never really thought about his brother in those terms. It would have been disloyal, he guessed, but with his own mother pointing it out, it was impossible to argue.

"I loved Jack," she said, fisting her hand against her chest. "When he died, I lost a piece of my heart I'll never get back. But I'm not blind to my children's faults just because I love them to distraction." Connie gave him a wistful smile. "When it came to adventure, there was no one better than Jack. But he never had the courage to love one woman and build a life with her. To face the everyday crises that crop up, to pay bills, get a mortgage, take the kids to the dentist. *That's* life, Sam. A real life with all the ups, downs, tears and laughter that come with it. That kind of thing terrified him and he did everything he could to avoid it."

Sam thought about that and realized his mother was right. Jack had always gone for the one-night stand kind of woman. The kind who hated commitment as much as he did himself.

"You had that courage once, Sam. When you married Lacy and began to build a life together." She sighed a little and stared into his eyes. "You walked away from that, and I'm not going to say now whether that was right or wrong because it's done and can't be undone. My question is, do you still have that courage, Sam? Do you still want that life with Lacy?"

The question hung in the air between them and seemed to reverberate inside him, as well. He looked at his mother, then at his father. At the room around them and the memories etched into the very walls. His life was here. It was time he picked it up and claimed it once and for all. He did want that life that he'd once been foolish enough to throw away. He wanted another chance to build what his parents had built.

He wasn't Jack. Sam wanted permanent. He wanted the everyday with the one woman who would make each single day special. All he had to do was find the way to make Lacy listen. To make her understand that he damn well loved her, and she loved him, too.

"Yeah, Mom," he said softly, reaching out to pull his mother close. "I do."

She hugged him hard—no more wary caution from her—and for the first time since he'd come back to Snow Vista, he really felt as if he was home again.

"You're *pregnant*?"

"Yes, and don't tell your brother."

"Not a word," Kristi swore, fingers crossing her heart, then flying up into a salute of solidarity. "How far along are you? Never mind. Can't be far. He's only been home a month. It *is* Sam's, right?"

Lacy gave her an exasperated look.

"Right, right," Kristi said, using both hands to wipe away her words, "it's Sam's. The idiot."

"That about covers how I'm feeling about him right now."

Lacy had been ranting about Sam for the past hour, and when news of the baby had slipped out, she'd had to swear her friend to silence. But she couldn't regret sharing her big secret with her best friend. It had felt too good to tell *someone*.

Lacy was still so furious she could hardly see straight, but mostly at herself, for falling for Sam's stories again. Seriously. *If you're going to make mistakes*, she thought, *at least have the good sense to make some new ones along the way.* But how could she have avoided letting herself be sucked back in? She still loved him. Though she was going to find a way to get over it. Maybe *she* should start reading those self-help books that Kristi was so addicted to. What she needed was a book called *How to Wipe That Man Out of Your Life.*

"What're you going to do?"

Lacy dropped into the closest chair and stared at the fire in her hearth. "I'm going to have a baby and never speak to your brother again."

"Hmm…" Kristi leaned into her own chair. "I applaud the sentiment, but it's gonna be tough. What with you both living here and all."

"He won't stay," Lacy muttered. "Soon enough, he'll be gone again, chasing his dead brother's dreams."

"I used to think Jack was the dummy, but I'm sorry to say," Kristi mused, "turns out Sam's the lucky winner there."

Lacy cringed a little. "I'm sorry. I shouldn't be dumping all of this on you. He's your brother. You shouldn't be in the middle."

"Are you kidding? In matters like these, it's all about girls versus boys as far as I'm concerned."

She smiled. "You're a good friend, Kristi."

"I could be better if you'd let me go kick Sam."

"No." Anger was now riding hand in hand with misery, and the two were so tangled up inside her, Lacy could hardly breathe. But she did know enough to realize that giving Sam any more attention at all would be just what he wanted. So she was going to ignore him. Forever.

Oh, for heaven's sake, how would she ever be able to

pull that off? It wouldn't be long before she'd be showing and Sam would know about the baby and…

"Maybe I'm the one who should move."

"Don't you dare," Kristi countered in a flash. "What
would I do here without you to talk to? Besides, you've
got my niece or nephew in there—" she waved one hand
at Lacy's tummy "—and I want to meet them."

"Yes, but—"

"Mostly, though," Kristi said smugly, "if you leave,
you let Sam think you were too afraid to stay in your
own home."

Oh, she didn't like the sound of that at all. Plus, the
truth was, Lacy didn't want to move. She loved her
cabin. She loved her job. She loved the mountain. She
loved *Sam*, damn it.

"Can your head actually explode?" she wondered
aloud.

"I hope not," Kristi said solemnly. "Now, why don't
we go out for dinner or something? Get your mind off
my idiot—er, brother."

Lacy smiled as she'd been meant to, but shook her
head. "No thanks. I just want to stay home and bury
my head under a pillow."

"Sounds like a plan." Kristi pushed up from the chair.
"I'll leave you to it."

Lacy got up, too, and wrapped her friend in a tight
hug. "Thanks. For everything."

"You bet. This'll work out, Lacy. You'll see." There
was a knock at the door and Kristi asked, "Want me to
get that and send whoever it is away?"

"God, yes. Thanks."

Kristi opened the door and Lacy heard Sam's voice
say "I want to talk to her."

"Surprise," Kristi shot back, "she doesn't want to talk to you."

Lacy groaned and went to face Sam because she couldn't put siblings at war over her. It was too soon, was all she could think. It had only been a few hours since that horrible scene at the top of the mountain. She needed a day or two or a hundred before she was willing to speak to Sam again. Yet it seemed fate didn't care about what she needed.

"It's okay, Kristi, I'll handle it."

"You sure?" Her friend's eyes narrowed in concern.

"Yeah, I'm fine." Of course she wasn't, but she wouldn't give Sam the satisfaction of knowing just how off balance she was with him here. She would be calm. Cool. Controlled, damn it!

"Okay, I'll leave," Kristi announced with a glare at Sam. "But I won't be far. Idiot."

"Thanks," he said wryly, "that's nice."

"Be grateful Lacy made me promise not to kick you," she called back over her shoulder.

Lacy watched him give his sister a dirty look, then grit his teeth as he turned around to face the door. Sadly, she didn't have enough time to slam it shut before he slapped one palm to it and held it open.

He was still wearing the black jacket and jeans. His dark hair still looked windblown and completely touchable. His eyes were shadowed, his mouth grim, and in spite of everything, her heart leaped and her body hummed with a desire that would probably never end. Mind and heart were at war inside her, but for her own good, for the sake of her baby, she had to be strong.

Behind him, she saw the soft, dying streaks of sunlight spearing through the pines. The dark green stalks of soon-to-bloom daffodils popped up all over her yard and the last of the snow lay in dwindling, dirty mounds.

"Lacy, you had your say on the mountain," Sam told her, dragging her gaze to his. "At least hear me out now."

"Why should I?"

He looked at her for a few long seconds, then admitted, "I can't think of a single damn reason. Do it anyway."

Sam walked into the main room and took a moment to gather himself. He looked around at the familiar space, the comfortable furnishings, the hominess of it all and felt his heart ease. Funny, he'd spent most of his life thinking of the mountain as home. But it was this place. It was *Lacy*.

Wherever she was, that was his home. He only hoped she would take him back.

An invisible fist tightened around his heart and gave a vicious squeeze. Was she still so furious she wouldn't listen to him? Wouldn't let him fix this? What could have been panic scratched at his guts, but he shoved it down, ignored it. He wouldn't fail at this, the most important thing he'd ever done. He'd make her listen. Make her understand and then make her admit she loved him, damn it.

Lacy walked into the room behind him, but stopped three feet away. She crossed her arms over her chest, lifted her chin in what could only be a fighting stance and said, "Say what you came to say, then leave."

She'd been crying. Her lashes were still wet, her face was flushed and her mouth trembled even as she made an attempt to firm it. *Bastard*, he thought, bringing her to this, and if he could have punched himself in the face, he would have. But it wouldn't have solved anything.

"First," he said tightly, "let's get this off the table. Keep your land. I don't want it."

Her eyebrows lifted into twin blond arches. "That's not what the newspaper reported."

"They were wrong." He pushed one hand through his hair. "Okay, I admit that I did have the idea for building a new beginner run on the backside of the mountain."

Her mouth tightened further into a grim slash that didn't bode well for Sam. But he kept going, determined to say everything that needed to be said.

"But Dad told me they'd deeded the property to you, so I let that idea go."

"How magnanimous of you."

Scowling, he snapped, "Damn it, Lacy, I didn't know you owned the land. When I found out, I changed my plans."

"And I'm supposed to take your word for that?"

"Believe me or not, doesn't matter," he countered, and took a step toward her. She didn't move away and he didn't know if that was sheer stubbornness or a willingness to listen. He took it as the latter. "The only thing you need to believe is that I love you."

Her eyes flickered with emotion but he couldn't tell if that was good or bad, so he kept talking. "Took me two damn years to realize what I had. What I lost. But I know now, we belong together, Lacy."

She huffed out a breath and shook her head. Her hands tightened on her own arms until her knuckles whitened, but she didn't speak. Didn't order him to get out. That had to mean something.

"I know I hurt you when I left."

She snorted. "You crushed me."

He winced and kept talking. "I did and I'm sorry for it. But even when we were first married, things were shaky between us. You kept waiting for me to disappoint you. To walk away, like your mother did."

"I was right, wasn't I?" She whispered it, but he heard and ached for her.

"Yeah, I guess you were. But you know, you always looked at what your mother did—leaving—as what love was really all about. So you thought I'd do what she did. You never really believed that I'd stay. Admit that much at least."

She took a breath and said, "To ease your guilt? Why would I? I can tell you that I wanted to believe you, but if I had believed, completely, your leaving would have killed me."

Pain slammed into the center of his chest and he deserved it for putting both of them through this.

"But I trusted you, Sam," she said, adding to the misery he felt now. "And you broke my heart."

Sunset was streaking across the sky outside, but inside, where the light was dim, shadowy and still, he could see the hurting in her summer-blue eyes.

"I know and I'll always regret that, wish I could go back and change it." His voice dropped into a husky whisper that tore at his throat even as her words clawed at his heart. "But, Lacy, your mother wasn't an example of love. Your father was. He *stayed*. He stayed with you. Right here. He lived through the unhappiness and never let it affect how he treated his daughter. That's the kind of love I'm offering you now."

A couple of long seconds ticked past as she considered what he said.

"You're right about my father," she agreed. "I never

thought about it like that, but you're right. She left. He stayed. He was lonely. Sad. But he stayed. *You* didn't."

"No." He hated admitting to that. "But I'm back now. And I'm not going anywhere."

She shook her head again, unwilling to take him at his word, and he only had himself to blame for it.

"I'm here forever, Lacy," he told her, willing her to believe. To trust. "I want a life with you. Children with you. I want to grow old and crotchety on this mountain and watch our kids and grandkids running Snow Vista."

She swayed a little and Sam took that as hope and moved another step closer. "If I have to spend the next ten years romancing you to get you to believe me, then that's what I'll do," he vowed. "I'll bring you flowers every day, dinner every night. I'll kiss you, touch you, make promises to you and eventually, you'll believe in me again."

"Will I?"

"Yeah," he said softly, a smile curving his mouth. "Because you love me, Lacy. As much as I love you."

She took a fast, shallow breath and held it for a long moment.

Sam looked at her standing there, her long hair loose and soft, her features tight, unsure, her eyes damp with tears, and his heart swelled until he thought it might burst from his chest.

"Lacy, I hurt you. I know that and if I could change the past I would. But all I can do is promise you tomorrow and all the tomorrows afterward." Breathing ragged, he took another step toward her. "You know, last night, after we talked, after I told you everything, I realized something I never had before."

"What?"

One word only, but he took that as a good sign, too.

"It wasn't just losing Jack that drove me from here—though that was devastating. I was scared. See, I loved you so much more than my own twin, the thought of losing you was unimaginable."

"Sam…"

"No," he said quickly, "just hear me out. I couldn't stand the thought of maybe losing you, as well. Seems stupid now, to leave you because I was afraid of losing you."

"Yeah," she agreed wryly. "It does."

"But leaving didn't stop the fear," he told her. "I still thought about you. Worried about you. *Loved* you. Staying with you is the only thing that can stop that fear. I know that now. I want to be with you. Dream with you, for however long we live." He took a long breath, let it out and said, "I want to risk the pain to have the love."

Lacy's heart was galloping in her chest. Her mind was reeling. She looked up into his eyes and knew that he was right. About everything. At the start of their marriage, she had been waiting for Sam to let her down. She'd kept her guard up, prepared to be hurt. As much as she'd loved Sam, she'd never really gone all in. She'd held a part of herself back. Always cautious.

She *had* forgotten that her father had always been there for her. In her pain over the loss of her mother, she'd refused to see that love doesn't always leave. Sometimes it stayed. And it was something to count on. To trust in. *That* was the love she wanted to believe in. The kind that never left. The kind that lasted forever.

Yes, she thought, looking up at him, Sam had made mistakes, but so had she. If she had been stronger in her own right, more self-confident, she might have forced him to talk to her in those days after Jack's death. They might have worked this out together. But she'd been half expecting him to leave, so when he did, she'd let it happen instead of fighting for what she wanted.

Now she was willing to fight.

He was watching her through those beautiful green eyes of his and she knew that the next step was hers to take. It always had been. She had to forgive. Had to believe. And looking into his eyes, she knew she did.

Love wasn't perfect. No doubt in the future they'd both make mistakes. But they would both stay. Together.

"You're right," she said, and watched as some of the tension drained out of him. "About a lot of things. But mostly," she said, "you're right that risking the pain is the only way to have the joy I feel when I'm with you."

"Will you risk it?" he asked, gaze never leaving hers. "Will you marry me again, Lacy? Will you trust me to be there for you and to always love you? Will you have my children and build a family with me?"

There it was, she thought. Everything she wanted, shiny and bright and laid at her feet. All she had to do was reach out and take it.

She held her hand out for his, and when his fingers closed around hers, she felt the warmth of him slide down inside and ease away the cold. "Yes, Sam. I'll marry you. I'll believe in you. And I'll love you all my life."

He gave a tug and she flew into his arms. As he held her, he whispered, "Thank God. I love you, Lacy. Now, always, forever, I love you."

"I love you, too, Sam. I always have. Always will." She nestled her head on his chest and listened to the thundering beat of his heart.

His arms encircling her, he asked softly, "What do you say we start making babies right away?"

A slow, satisfied smile crossed her face as she leaned

back to look up at him. "You can cross that one off your to-do list, Sam."

"What do you—" Understanding dawned and his eyes widened even as his jaw dropped. "You mean... are you...already?"

She nodded, waiting for the pleasure to ease past the shock. It didn't take long. His grin spread across his face and lit his eyes with the kind of joy she had once dreamed of seeing. Reality was so much better.

"We're going to have a great life," he promised her as one hand dropped to tenderly cup her flat belly.

She laid her hand over his and said, "We've already started."

Then he kissed her and Lacy's world opened up into a bright, beautiful place.

Epilogue

Lacy had a private room in the maternity ward at McKay-Dee Hospital in Ogden. Outside, it was snowing, but inside, there was a celebration going on.

Sam looked down at his wife, cuddling their newborn son, and felt everything in him surge with happiness. Contentment. The past few months had been full and busy and *great*. The restaurant opened in the fall and was already packed daily. The gift shop was a huge hit not only with the tourists, but also with the local artisans, and the lodge addition was nearly ready to take in guests.

But best of all was the time spent with Lacy. Rediscovering just how good they were together. They were living at her cabin, though they'd added so many rooms to the place, it was barely recognizable now. There were four more bedrooms, a couple of baths and a country kitchen that Lacy rarely wanted to leave. They had plans to fill that cabin with kids and laughter, and they'd gotten their start today.

"You were amazing," he told her, bending down to kiss her forehead, the tip of her nose and then her lips.

Lacy smiled up at him. "Our son is amazing. Just look at him, Sam. Isn't he beautiful?"

"Just like his mom," Sam said, trailing the tip of one finger along his son's cheek. He never would have believed how deeply, how completely, you could love a person not even an hour old. He was a *father*. And a very lucky man.

"He's got your hair and my eyes. Isn't that incredible? His own little person but a part of both of us." She sighed happily and kissed her son's forehead.

"How are you feeling?" Worry colored his words, but he could be forgiven for that. Hadn't he just watched her work and struggle for eight hours to give birth? A harrowing experience he was in no hurry to repeat. "Tired? Hungry?"

She laughed a little at that, caught Sam's hand in hers and gave it a squeeze. "Okay, yeah, I could eat one of Maria's steak sandwiches and swallow it whole. But I feel *great*. I have so much energy, I could get up and ski Bear Run."

The fastest, most dangerous slope at Snow Vista. Shaking his head, he said, "Yeah. You can forget about that for a while."

Lacy grinned and shrugged. "I suppose, but I'm really not tired." Narrowing her gaze on him, she said, "But you're exhausted. You should go home and rest."

"I'm not going anywhere without you." Thankfully, the hospital provided cots for new fathers to sleep on in their wives' rooms. Though he'd have stayed, even if he'd had to sleep in the chair by her bed. He kissed her again, kissed the top of his son's head, and then straightened and threw a glance at the door. "The family's waiting to come in. You ready to face them?"

"Absolutely."

He walked over, waved in the crowd of Wyatts and moved to the head of Lacy's bed as everyone crowded around. His parents were beaming, his father clutching an impossibly bright purple teddy bear, his mother carrying a vase of sunshine-yellow roses. His sister, Kristi, was there, holding her husband Tony's hand. The two of them had finally married last May, and Kristi was already pregnant with their first child.

"He's gorgeous," Connie Wyatt exclaimed.

"Handsome boy," Bob agreed.

"What's his name?" Kristi asked, looking from Lacy to Sam.

He looked down at his beautiful wife and smiled when she said, "You tell them, Sam."

He dropped one hand to Lacy's shoulder, linking them, making them the unit they'd become. Sam looked at his family and said, "His name is Jackson William Wyatt. Named for Jack and for Lacy's dad."

Sam watched his mother's eyes well with tears and she didn't try to stop them as they spilled along her cheeks even as she gave them both a proud smile. "Jack would be pleased. We are, aren't we, honey?"

Bob Wyatt dropped one arm around his wife and pulled her in tight. "We are. It's a good thing you've done, you two."

Sam watched the family talk in excited whispers and half shouts. He saw Lacy hand baby Jack over to his mother and watched as she turned to Sam's father and the two of them cuddled and cooed at their first grandchild.

Life was good. Couldn't be better. All that was missing, he thought with a lingering touch of sorrow, was his brother. He wished that Jack could know somehow that they had survived his loss. Found happiness, in spite of missing him.

A flicker of movement caught Sam's eye and he turned his head, shooting a look at the corner of the room, where the watery winter sun painted a pillar of golden light.

Sam's breath caught.

Jack was there, in the light, a part of it. Heart thudding in his chest, Sam could only stare at his twin in disbelief. The buzz of conversation around him softened and drifted away as he and his twin stared at each other from across the room, across the chasm between life and death.

Jack nodded, as if he understood just what Sam was feeling. Then he gave his twin a slow, wide smile, just as he used to. And in moments, as Sam watched, Jack drifted away with the last of the light until the corner of the room was empty and dark again.

"Sam?" Lacy called his name, and still bemused by what he'd seen, he turned to her, a half smile curving his mouth. "Are you okay?"

He glanced back at the corner of the room. Had it happened? Or was it wishful thinking? Did it matter? Jack was a part of them, always would be. Maybe he'd just found a way to let Sam know that he was okay, too.

Turning back to Lacy, Sam let go of the last of his pain and welcomed the joy he was being offered.

"I'm more than okay," he assured her. "Everything's perfect."

Then he turned his back on the past and stepped into the future with his wife and son.

* * * * *

MILLS & BOON®
Hardback – March 2015

ROMANCE

The Taming of Xander Sterne	Carole Mortimer
In the Brazilian's Debt	Susan Stephens
At the Count's Bidding	Caitlin Crews
The Sheikh's Sinful Seduction	Dani Collins
The Real Romero	Cathy Williams
His Defiant Desert Queen	Jane Porter
Prince Nadir's Secret Heir	Michelle Conder
Princess's Secret Baby	Carol Marinelli
The Renegade Billionaire	Rebecca Winters
The Playboy of Rome	Jennifer Faye
Reunited with Her Italian Ex	Lucy Gordon
Her Knight in the Outback	Nikki Logan
Baby Twins to Bind Them	Carol Marinelli
The Firefighter to Heal Her Heart	Annie O'Neil
Thirty Days to Win His Wife	Andrea Laurence
Her Forbidden Cowboy	Charlene Sands
The Blackstone Heir	Dani Wade
After Hours with Her Ex	Maureen Child

MEDICAL

Tortured by Her Touch	Dianne Drake
It Happened in Vegas	Amy Ruttan
The Family She Needs	Sue MacKay
A Father for Poppy	Abigail Gordon

MILLS & BOON®
Large Print – March 2015

ROMANCE

A Virgin for His Prize	Lucy Monroe
The Valquez Seduction	Melanie Milburne
Protecting the Desert Princess	Carol Marinelli
One Night with Morelli	Kim Lawrence
To Defy a Sheikh	Maisey Yates
The Russian's Acquisition	Dani Collins
The True King of Dahaar	Tara Pammi
The Twelve Dates of Christmas	Susan Meier
At the Chateau for Christmas	Rebecca Winters
A Very Special Holiday Gift	Barbara Hannay
A New Year Marriage Proposal	Kate Hardy

HISTORICAL

Darian Hunter: Duke of Desire	Carole Mortimer
Rescued by the Viscount	Anne Herries
The Rake's Bargain	Lucy Ashford
Unlaced by Candlelight	Various
The Warrior's Winter Bride	Denise Lynn

MEDICAL

A Secret Shared...	Marion Lennox
Flirting with the Doc of Her Dreams	Janice Lynn
The Doctor Who Made Her Love Again	Susan Carlisle
The Maverick Who Ruled Her Heart	Susan Carlisle
After One Forbidden Night...	Amber McKenzie
Dr Perfect on Her Doorstep	Lucy Clark

MILLS & BOON®
Hardback – April 2015

ROMANCE

The Billionaire's Bridal Bargain	Lynne Graham
At the Brazilian's Command	Susan Stephens
Carrying the Greek's Heir	Sharon Kendrick
The Sheikh's Princess Bride	Annie West
His Diamond of Convenience	Maisey Yates
Olivero's Outrageous Proposal	Kate Walker
The Italian's Deal for I Do	Jennifer Hayward
Virgin's Sweet Rebellion	Kate Hewitt
The Millionaire and the Maid	Michelle Douglas
Expecting the Earl's Baby	Jessica Gilmore
Best Man for the Bridesmaid	Jennifer Faye
It Started at a Wedding...	Kate Hardy
Just One Night?	Carol Marinelli
Meant-To-Be Family	Marion Lennox
The Soldier She Could Never Forget	Tina Beckett
The Doctor's Redemption	Susan Carlisle
Wanted: Parents for a Baby!	Laura Iding
His Perfect Bride?	Louisa Heaton
Twins on the Way	Janice Maynard
The Nanny Plan	Sarah M. Anderson

MILLS & BOON®
Large Print – April 2015

ROMANCE

Taken Over by the Billionaire	Miranda Lee
Christmas in Da Conti's Bed	Sharon Kendrick
His for Revenge	Caitlin Crews
A Rule Worth Breaking	Maggie Cox
What The Greek Wants Most	Maya Blake
The Magnate's Manifesto	Jennifer Hayward
To Claim His Heir by Christmas	Victoria Parker
Snowbound Surprise for the Billionaire	Michelle Douglas
Christmas Where They Belong	Marion Lennox
Meet Me Under the Mistletoe	Cara Colter
A Diamond in Her Stocking	Kandy Shepherd

HISTORICAL

Strangers at the Altar	Marguerite Kaye
Captured Countess	Ann Lethbridge
The Marquis's Awakening	Elizabeth Beacon
Innocent's Champion	Meriel Fuller
A Captain and a Rogue	Liz Tyner

MEDICAL

It Started with No Strings...	Kate Hardy
One More Night with Her Desert Prince...	Jennifer Taylor
Flirting with Dr Off-Limits	Robin Gianna
From Fling to Forever	Avril Tremayne
Dare She Date Again?	Amy Ruttan
The Surgeon's Christmas Wish	Annie O'Neil

MILLS & BOON®

Why shop at millsandboon.co.uk?

Each year, thousands of romance readers find their perfect read at millsandboon.co.uk. That's because we're passionate about bringing you the very best romantic fiction. Here are some of the advantages of shopping at www.millsandboon.co.uk:

* **Get new books first**—you'll be able to buy your favourite books one month before they hit the shops

* **Get exclusive discounts**—you'll also be able to buy our specially created monthly collections, with up to 50% off the RRP

* **Find your favourite authors**—latest news, interviews and new releases for all your favourite authors and series on our website, plus ideas for what to try next

* **Join in**—once you've bought your favourite books, don't forget to register with us to rate, review and join in the discussions

Visit **www.millsandboon.co.uk**
for all this and more today!